THE GRIMOIRE

Published by J K Easter

THE GRIMOIRE

J K Easter

Published by J K Easter

The Grimoire

A novel by J K Easter

First published in 2013

Published by J K Easter

ISBN - 978-1-919663-11-1 (Paperback)

First edition 2013

Cover image designed by Brian Allen: www.flylanddesigns.com

Printing by Lightening Source

The Author

Jason Kurt Easter, born 1973, works as a health professional in Gibraltar. He's a biologist and naturalist, but has a special interest in folklore, mythology and fantastical literature. The Grimoire is Jason's debut young adult fantasy novel.

Jason embarked on postgraduate study in 2010, feeling the need to learn more about the writing craft. He completed his Master of Arts in Professional Writing in 2012, and is currently working on a variety of fiction and non-fiction projects.

For more information please visit: www.jkeaster.com

This book
is dedicated
to Aleksandra
for her
encouragement,
belief, love
and support.

1

Tenderfoots

Today was a day like yesterday. The youngsters rattled and shouted and Therolius was in an unsettled mood. There was something on his mind. Paper planes assisted by magic swooped and swerved, climbed and dived, blinked different colours; some even changed shape. They popped, banged, vanished, reappeared, turned to dust and burst into flames. The behaviour was a little immature for the tenderfoots of this prefatory class, especially as they were all twelve and about to advance to apprentices of magic. They were the wizards of tomorrow.

The noise in the classroom had reached an alarming level. The room was tense. Therolius sat at his desk, elbows extended, resting his face in cupped hands. A curtain of long grey hair touched with white and black tips draped until it eventually rested on the table like a bridal train. His crumpled black hat did not look like the customary half-moon; it had flopped over to one side.

The students known as tenderfoots, persisted with their

lively actions shouting at an increasing rate and banging hard on their roll-top desks. His head began to thump like a drum and he couldn't take much more. His disappointment at their behaviour increased and became anger. He rose slowly from the comfort of his chair, causing a screeching and dragging sound as it scraped across the floor. One young girl noticed this and her plane plummeted to the floor as if the pilot had executed an emergency eject. On the far side of the room a boy sat still, smiling, showing his innocent dimples. His plane landed gracefully on his beech-wood desk.

'SHOW SOME RESPECT FOR THE OVERLORD! SHUT UP! SHUT UP AND SIT DOWN!' the wizard shouted, spittle suspending from his lower lip like bungees. His arms were extended horizontally like a preacher; his head stooped. Straight hair fell in an orderly fashion to his shoulders and a traditional wizard's hat sat on his head. The din in the room subsided to a low chatter. He wiped his mouth. 'And the same goes for all you wands! Honestly, you should know better.' His displeased voice echoed. The wands were hidden in blue velvet bags that hung on hooks at the back of the class, each with the tenderfoot's name embroidered on it. He cleared his throat and a couple of wands blew raspberries at him, but he ignored them.

The room gradually fell silent; the paper planes became lifeless. Some had landed hard, others gracefully drifted to the floor aided by a draft. Therolius, the supreme wizard, also called the Overlord, looked up and tucked his hair behind his ears, first one side, and then the other. He took a few deep breaths and composed himself straightening his well-fitting, vivid blue tunic decorated with gold trimmings.

'There… That's better.'

The classroom was now so quiet it allowed Therolius to continue. 'So much better!' He walked over to the chalkboard and wiped clear the previous day's lesson notes with a swipe of his wand.

'As I touched on yesterday, we need to learn the basics of magic in order to understand it and become proficient spell-casters. At the end of term you,' he paused whilst pointing to three tenderfoots, 'will become apprentices of magic; the beginning of a respectable yet difficult craft.'

The wizard turned and faced the chalkboard. 'Today we will learn about spell-casting.' Then he picked up a piece of chalk and wrote the word "spell-casting" in large bold letters. He didn't want to use his wand this time.

'Can anyone tell me the three forms of spell-casting?' he said, then twisted his body towards the tenderfoots. An array of hands shot up. He picked a freckled and ginger-haired girl with thick braces.

'Arcane, Witchcraft and Psychic!' suggested the girl who then bit her lip, wondering whether she was right.

'Correct, Miss Evercrest.'

The girl's face changed in a flash from unease to self-satisfaction.

Therolius began to chalk the board. 'Arcane, as we know it, is the scientific manipulation of natural energies. This is achieved through the combination of voice, hand movements, and physical energies.' A cough sprang from the back. Therolius glanced over his shoulder: 'Any objections?'

The class remained silent.

He carried on writing, this drawing a large "W" on the board. 'Witchcraft involves tapping into these natural energies in order to release them into the physical plane of our world. This is achieved through meditation, the burning of candles, chanting and repeating incantations. Fortunately this is rarely seen in Sintar. It is classed as the forbidden craft. It involves herbal preparations as well as some of the most horrid rituals.'

The class maintained silence, yet some eyes wandered. Therolius was pleased and began to relax. He continued to write on the board.

'Psychic is the manipulation of the world by powers harnessed through the mind. This type of spell-casting requires intense discipline and focus and is a gift. You either have it, or you don't.'

'Is this the same as spiritual spell-casting?' someone asked.

Therolius pointed high in the air with the stick of chalk.

'Ahh! Interesting question! At least someone is listening.' He turned to face the tenderfoots. 'Well? Can anyone answer Mr Zalbar's question?'

Therolius was surprised the class had become so silent and biddable. Only moments ago they had seemed uncontrollable. Eyes were still darting back and forth as Tenderfoots looked to each other for answers.

'Well in answer to your question, Mr Zalbar I would say that this is not really classed as spell-casting.'

'Why not?' asked Zalbar.

'*The Grimoire* tells us that wizards are not psychics. Psychics are spiritual in a sense yes, but it's difficult to explain. I would say it's more of a... Religion.'

'I don't entirely understand,' said Zalbar. He looked down for a second in thought and then glanced up.

'Well, what I mean is that if wizards have the power to cast spells with their minds then that would make them psychic.' Therolius placed the piece of chalk delicately on his table and brushed his hands together releasing a cloud of dust. 'I think what you refer to is a form of "spiritual spell-casting." It concerns itself with the manipulation of the energy derived from parallel spirit planes. Whether it means communicating with, or summoning, spirits or phantoms, or simply tapping into the magical plane beyond us, wizards can't do it. It's an urban myth.'

'But wizards *can* do it. They *must* be able to.'

'What do you mean *can* do it? Wizards can't! They

need wands to perform magic. The wand is their conduit that taps into the magical plane. In fact wizards need their wands to perform any magical action. The wand is also a guide and friend for wizards that lets them choose wisely and to learn from it. It has always been like that, and will continue to be so.'

'Then psychics are better than wizards because they don't need wands, they use their minds.'

The questioning from the youngster was starting to irritate Therolius. He felt the lesson slipping away from his control because of the innocent probing of a child.

'They are different, but they aren't better! Psychics fall under the school's guidance as aids to wizards. There is no comparing them with wizards and they can't perform magic.'

'So unlike psychics, wizards experience two lives in one, the magical and the normal?'

'Yes, in essence this is true.' Therolius hoped the questioning would stop at that, but it didn't.

Zalbar touched his chin; and pressed on with his inquisition. 'So is it possible for wizards to also have the power of manipulation using their minds? Even the possibility of,' he paused for a split-second, '… not even needing wands?'

An uncomfortable tension pervaded the room and some tenderfoot eyes opened very wide. The atmosphere was tense. Soft chatter broke the silence. The boy smiled to the point where he was beaming. Therolius's blood pressure rose. This sort of talk was unheard of and unacceptable. He had to put a stop to it.

'I think this has gone far enough. There is no need for disrespecting our wizarding ways. If we revert back to what I was saying.' The wizard picked up the chalk from the table and turned back towards the board.

'—So there are basically two types of spell-casting or magic?' the boy cut in, not willing to drop the topic.

Therolius turned abruptly. 'I thought I said—'

'I believe there are the manipulative and the harnessing sides to spell-casting. I've been reading up on this.'

'I'm not going to answer—'

'So it must be possible to combine the two,' Zalbar persisted as if he were talking to himself.

'Impossible! *The Grimoire* states that this is not possible.' Therolius retorted in an irritated tone.

'But what would happen if it was, Sir?' The boy shuffled in his seat and leant on his desk in a somewhat haughty manner. 'If a person *could* find a way to join the two.'

Zalbar glared at the Overlord with intent that some might have attached the word evil to. It made Therolius uncomfortable, and he walked around his desk tapping it three times with a finger as he spoke. 'Harnessing varieties of magic is harmless; it does not change the natural order of things.'

'So what's all the fuss about then? You say it's not

possible, but it clearly is.'

The wizard shook his head with closed eyes and took a deep, consoling breath. 'Manipulative spell-casting in its extreme forms, Mr Zalbar,' he said, putting an authoritative stress on the name, 'involves opening parallel dimensions. This can disturb the natural routes of magic. These dimensions have to be treated with care. For the "harnessing magic" to reside in the physical form, in our world, in one plane, would take immense power and aptitude. Not even the most gifted of "bloods" would ever attempt this. Besides, not many wizards would know how to combine the energies, let alone contain them within their physical form.' There was a slight tremor in the wizard's lower lip.

'So it is possible,' muttered Zalbar in a low, but audible, tone.

'I would have to disagree,' Therolius lied. 'Tampering with magic is a dangerous endeavour. Who knows what could happen? It's more likely that a wizard would not be able to contain the immense energy. The wizard would... puff into smoke.' He had lied again. He could not believe he was allowing this discourse. 'Magic should be respected, like a religion! And on that topic I think you should not pursue this matter any further, Mr Zalbar. Just concentrate on passing your prefatory. You need to pass this exam if you have any ambitions of becoming a wizard.'

'But I have read extracts from *The Grimoire* and—'

Zalbar remained persistent.

'You have read interpretations of *The Grimoire*, made by the various Overlords before me. Don't assume you know everything, Mr Zalbar, because you don't,' said Therolius, in a firm and threatening voice.

The Grimoire was a subject close to Therolius's heart and his life's work had involved trying to understand its powers and the text. By now he'd lost volition and was reluctant to carry on with the lesson.

'I think class is over for today.'

The faces of the tenderfoots oozed bewilderment, yet one seemed happy with the decision. The bell rang and a little girl cheered. The class shot an unkindly glance at her.

'Come now, class is over. Make your way over to Gimera Zelus for your Basic Potions class. Remember your prefatory is in two weeks. You need to prep yourself and listen carefully to your wands. They will guide you. That includes you, Mr Zalbar!'

Therolius was unnerved and still fidgety but tried his best to hide it. The discussion had raised the spectre of an old threat. Could history repeat? He hoped fervently that it wouldn't, and then left the classroom in a troubled mood.

2

The Grimoire

Therolius walked slowly down the corridor towards his chambers, his mind unsettled by Zalbar's questioning. 'This can't be good,' he muttered, 'a tenderfoot questioning the Overlord. Why persist when I made it clear he was wrong?'

What worried Therolius was Zalbar's aptitude despite his outlandish impulse. Why persist in class? Was he trying to prove something?

He thought hard, but couldn't come up with a satisfactory answer. Reflecting on Zalbar's time at the orphanage didn't help either. The magical gift did not grace the orphanage as often as one would like. Zalbar had had problems fitting in with other children and Therolius knew that a gift needed the proper schooling. Since he had brought him to the school he had noticed Zalbar made no effort to fit in. Zalbar was a natural and was advancing quickly, but perhaps too quickly. Therolius sighed at his decision to admit him to school, opening the child up to the realms of knowledge. The quick grasp of magic he was endowed with was only ever found in "bloods", the naturals, the blue-blooded, but Zalbar wasn't one of them. He wasn't even a pure blood, a wizard born of two "bloods". So where had his gift come from?

The corridor was dark and faintly lit. Echoes of the wizard's footsteps rebounded off the walls. The atmosphere was cold and uninviting. Therolius stopped and lifted up his knee to prevent the books he was carrying from slipping to the floor, reaffirming his grip on a tower of arcane literature. A whisper sprang from the shadows. He stood still, eyes travelling left and right, before he cautiously glanced backwards. There was nothing. He continued forward, this time taking quicker steps, then longer steps. Whispers again leapt out from behind him, now louder, but not clearer. The wizard's cloak floated on the floor as he hurried the last metre of the corridor, inserting his key, opening the door and anxiously entering his office, slamming the door firmly behind him. The lock clicked shut as he leaned against the wooden door with closed eyes whilst regaining his breath. He approached the table and dumped the books on it. A faint glow in the pit of his fireplace was gradually fading.

'*Ignis!*' Therolius barked pointing his wand at the cast iron fire-basket. Spiralling flames appeared, darting over the gold pot and dancing along the brickwork. The room was now warmly lit. He could feel the warmth cover his old hands as he approached the fire. He rubbed them together before showing the fire his palms. Another whisper filled the room. He turned and struggled to pull a thick elm wand from out of his pocket, which for a short moment stuck to the inner lining. The whisper disappeared. Therolius walked to the centre of his office and slowly pivoted in a circle, attentively; he could sense someone was with him. Then a large silhouette appeared in front of the wizard, followed by a smaller figure.

'Zalbar?' The wizard was shocked for a moment, but then relaxed and lowered his wand. 'My boy you gave me quite a fright! Don't you know it's improper to creep up on your elders? You'll give them a heart attack!' He turned again, chuckling towards his desk. He placed his wand down and then walked to the fire. He bent and picked up a brass stoker and prodded the fire a few times releasing sparkles from the ash.

Zalbar had his hands behind his back, but then revealed them brandishing a thin, curly, dark-tanned wand. He pointed it at the wizard who was still poking the fire. 'Sorry Overlord… I have a habit of doing that.'

'There is also the question of how you got in—'

'*Exanimo*,' said Zalbar, in a lengthy whisper and the room shuddered for a second. A sharp breeze covered Therolius. There was a large window in the room and it rattled, as the ends of the curtains lifted. The fire flickered violently. Suddenly Therolius could no longer feel the warmth; it felt wintry. He couldn't turn around. In fact he could not move at all. He couldn't talk, but managed to roll his eyes, until he focused on his wand. Then his lips fused together and his mouth disappeared.

Zalbar looked at Therolius's wand and then tutted. 'Great spell isn't it? One I tweaked myself with a little help. Made it better in fact. Made it useful!'

He tilted his head whilst tucking away a small book that protruded from his left trouser pocket. The wizard tried to speak, but was unable to. Zalbar's greasy fringe fell onto his forehead, and he attended to it slowly.

Zalbar noticed a large, elaborately carved door about six feet from the wizard's desk. It was married with a wooden lintel, surrounded by forest leaves carved in oak. Its iron hatch was loosely fastened and as he looked Zalbar noticed a subtle green glow radiate from it, piercing through the unaligned gaps and hinges. Zalbar examined both Therolius and the green glow.

'Ahhh... So that's where you keep it restrained,' said Zalbar with a hint of sarcasm.

The wizard attempted to talk, but it was hopeless. His eyes darted from one side to the other like a chameleon's.

Zalbar puckered his lips and tapped the end of his chin a few times with his wand, then laughed deeply and villainously.

'Go on; do it. Do it...' urged Zalbar's wand.

'When the time is right,' he replied.

'The time is now,' the wand said. 'Now, now, now!'

Zalbar's scheming pale face and rosy cheeks looked anything but innocent. Despite the well-groomed and sculptured schoolboy hair and neatly ironed shirt and trousers, he was far from a conforming or endearing presence. He was half the size of the wizard, but that didn't hinder his malevolent intention. It wasn't his size that startled or worried Therolius. He felt uncomfortable and panicky at the boy's strength and magical aptitude. Zalbar stepped closer and was now equidistant between Therolius and the greenly lit door.

'It's a paralysis spell, Overlord. As you must have figured out, I've stunned you. Me, a boy, has stunned *you*, the great wizard. Who would have thought a tenderfoot could ever stun the Overlord.' He flicked his head backwards and let out a victorious laugh, his boy-pitched tone not fitting the attempt. 'It won't last long, Therolius. I'll be out of here quicker than lightning, after I get what I came for, of course.' His gaze was fixed on the door. 'Most people fail to notice my...' he paused for a split second whilst walking to the door, '... Inner wizard. But you are more observant than most. Must be why you're the Overlord. I could see you flinch at my questions in class. I just needed you to admit that it was possible; and in a roundabout way you did.'

Zalbar lowered his wand and again scratched his chin. He whirled round, as if pirouetting on one foot and raised his wand aiming it at Therolius. He sauntered over, closer to the wizard, so close he could smell the old man's fear. He pointed his wand right between Therolius's eyes. 'And it IS possible!' he said, growling with insanity.

Noticing the wizard beginning to turn blue, Zalbar tutted: 'A blue-blood turning blue. Now isn't that funny?' He chuckled, pulling his head back, but immediately lunged forward a second time. 'Remember this face, Overlord; you'd be best not to forget it. *Alcedo imbellis!*' he spat at the wizard's face.

Therolius could smell Zalbar's breath. It was revolting, and quite the opposite of his angelic appearance.

'There, you can speak, but don't try to shout. Nobody will hear you.'

The Overlord's mouth reappeared. 'Zel... Zel—'

'No use.' He could see the wizard was calling his wand. 'He's not going to help you. Like I said, I've altered the spell a little here... And there.'

'Why? Re...lease me...or I'll—'

'—Or you'll what?'

Therolius didn't answer.

'I thought as much.'

There was a pause and then Therolius realised his speech had returned to normal.

'It's not possible. A tenderfoot has never been able to alter spells. Not unless...' Shock swiftly took hold of the wizard. His face didn't need a paralysis spell. He was transfixed and felt winded at the same time.

Zalbar smiled, beaming confidence through his blue eyes. 'Yes, your suspicion is correct.'

'But how was it that I—'

'Didn't know?' He finished Therolius's sentence and paced around before halting in front of the door. 'You simply didn't do your research well. You stopped just where you thought it ended. And that is where it all began!' Zalbar's temper was rising, but he took a couple of deep and composing breaths.

'Yeah. You didn't do it well did you?' Zalbar's wand added.

'Will you shut up!' Zalbar shook his wand. 'I said leave this to me.' Then he looked back at Therolius. 'The poor and disadvantaged will always be mistreated and overlooked by society. It only takes the Overlord to save the day. I hated Oliver Twist! What a cliché,' he hissed with disgust. 'What you need to be concerned with is that I know who I am, and what I am destined to become. Wizards at my age until now never existed.'

'You're no wizard!' Therolius was firm and precise.

'Oh, that's where you are wrong. For starters, there's this situation.' Zalbar gestured with his wand, waving it back and forth between Therolius and himself. 'And the second thing is that I don't need a piece of parchment from the school saying I'm a WIZARD! I simply am one.' He straightened his shirt, tending to his cuffs. 'And that's what scares you isn't it, Therolius? Oh, and there's another piece of information that may interest you. A little birdie told me that a relation of mine was involved in the revolt of the hunchbacks. Very interesting and I wonder who that could be. Someone you knew perhaps.'

The wizard's head suddenly felt heavy, his chest was tight and for a short moment he felt dizzy and confused. His mouth was dry and his heart started to pound. He began wriggling. Some movement had returned.

'Seems to be wearing off quicker than I expected, hmm.'

'I told you you needed more time,' said his wand.

'Shut up!' he snapped again at his wand.

Zalbar grabbed the door handle and turned it quickly.

The wizard muttered before shouting to the boy. 'Zalbar... Don't you dare!' He swallowed hard; and his throat was sore. But he could feel a sense of control returning.

Without haste Zalbar opened the door and the green light shone into the wizard's chambers. Zalbar shot the wizard a triumphant look before entering the forbidden room and slamming the door behind him.

'Wake up... Wake up will you?' The wizard shouted in a hoarse voice. His wand was quiet; then it began to mutter unclear words.

'ZELIUS! WAKE UP!'

The wand started to twitch on the floor. Then it darted

around as if it were being pulled on a thread, dragging along the table in wild directions. It moved closer to the edge and the wizard pleaded: 'ZELIUS! Now is not the time to sleep. WAKE… UP!' The wand fell to the floor, hitting the slate stone slabs. Suddenly the wand elevated itself off the floor and hovered. Therolius began to regain his movements and found that the spell had now worn off entirely. His hands became untied and the wand whizzed into his hand. Therolius spoke in a loud and resonant tone whilst pointing at the door.

'*Cogitatio ablego!*' A green light exuded from the Overlord's wand, individual streams of spiralled light pierced through the door. The green glow in the room became a vivid emerald.

Zalbar began to wail. Therolius's face changed and he winced at the suffering and torment he was causing, as if he were torturing an innocent boy. The wail turned to a high-pitched scream. Therolius was forced to look towards the fire, away from the door, in discomfort and disgust at what he was doing. He had no choice. His arm remained extended towards the door, the green light still pouring from the tip of his wand. The light began to turn white and the screams became unbearable. Therolius felt empty, bearing the ordeal, sharing the pain, but it had to be done. He couldn't let him leave. He had to ensure the safety of The Grimoire. He would rather live up to his oath as Overlord and die protecting the book if need be.

'Sorry... My boy. Your innocence will fool nobody ever again, for they will never see your face. And in that, ironically, they may see what you really are: a void; an absence.' The screams lasted a short time before a sudden and final force of energy shot from the Overlord's wand. Then a long-winded and airy hiss ensued as the light from the emerald faded to a pastel glimmer. Therolius lowered his wand and a dark ash cloud came wafting through the door. A curly, dark-tanned wand hovered in the cloud.

'We will meet again wizard!'

Then the cloud and wand imploded causing the window in Therolius's room to smash into tiny shards.

Therolius fell to his knees. He wiped his watery eyes with a sleeve; his face was pale, blank and lifeless. It was a while before he summoned the strength to lift himself off the floor. When he did he walked over to the door to the room, opened it and walked in. It was small, but just the right size to house the prize. Mounted on a shiny brass moulded lectern was The Grimoire, the textbook of all magic. The large leather book had four small pearls at each corner set in a raised border. The front and back covers were fastened shut by three shiny brass ornamental clasps. The pages were edged in gilt. Therolius ran his hand down the cover and sighed. As he did this he noticed a small book on the floor at the foot of the lectern. He picked it up and opened it. A loud screech erupted from the pages. Instinctively he dropped the book, which closed in mid air before falling to the floor. He stooped and picked it up and examined the cover; turning it from front to back. On the front cover it read:

This is the binding journal of Geldahar Zalbar.

An inexplicable and almost overwhelming fear swept through Therolius's being. He tucked the book into his tunic pocket and whispered to himself as he left: *What have you done Zalbar? What have you done?*

3

A Special Wand

Fizbar dusted a firmly fixed certificate on his wall with a feathery duster whilst sniggering to himself. It had hung there for more than two months all alone on the vast white space behind the desk in his office. He stared at his name written in big, old fashioned lettering, then traced his finger over the letters with a feeling of merriment combined with pure contentment. He felt the euphoria of his achievement, as if he had just been given his result by the Order of Wizards. It had been worth all the effort and he closed his eyes for several seconds; then childishly opened one eye, hoping it wasn't a dream. The bold black letters still read:

The Sintar School of Magic
This Diploma of Wizardry is awarded to
Fizbar Trundle
Having followed an approved programme in
Arcane Magic and Potions

Fizbar was a small, thin young man who had lived at Sintar all of the sixteen years since his birth. An incipient goatee emerging on the end of his slender chin was barely visible. His large brown eyes didn't match his black, shoulder-length hair. He was thin and lanky, but most boys his age were the same. The only broad-shouldered ones were brutes, sports-persons or manual labourers. Fizbar was equipped with magic so he felt he didn't need to run, and he had no cause to be a brute. He was now a wizard. It was an accomplishment and a respected one. The school's golden logo flickered on the bottom left of the large cream parchment. His face lit up as he sat behind his small oval desk and took off his small red pointed hat, placing it down in front of him. He stared at it and smiled at the emblem. He was a wizard of the first order and a gold hollow circle sat in the middle of his hat and a fancy designed *1* centred inside was decorated with three small circles that represented the three forms of spell-casting. His thoughts galloped away into consideration of advanced levels before these were dampened by realisation of the impediment of the seven ranks standing in his way.

'Overlord... Yes!' He paused, 'I'm going to be Overlord!' But his aspirations were further dampened by a simple fact.

'Running away with yourself again, Fizbar?' A polished voice manifested very close to Fizbar. He crumpled his brow focusing hard on the bookcases. 'You have to be a "blood" to become Overlord. Possessing a natural gift of magic very few wizards are adorned with.'

'A little dreaming never harmed anyone,' replied Fizbar. He knew that Overlord was a position he could never fulfil. Therolius Delrunt had been Overlord for a hundred years and wasn't going anywhere soon; at least he wasn't showing any signs of it. 'Archmage then?' Fizbar suggested an alternative. 'Gimera Zelus won't be Archmage forever, and Therolius has to have a successor one day. Possibilities will arise.'

'Which you will have no chance of procuring! You're not a "blood" for starters and Gimera is a lot younger than Therolius,' the voice added in a lecturing fashion.

'Yes I know! But accidents can also happen,' he giggled.

'I am going to ignore that remark.' The voice seemed appalled at that comment.

'Don't dispirit a wizard; it's not your job.'

'A wizard you are, but this is just the beginning of your elemental journey,' said the voice. 'And it will be quite a journey.'

'As my magical guide you're supposed to cheer me up; support my drive for excellence.'

'And as your guide it's also my duty to be realistic and impede any hasty decisions and dampen foolhardy aspirations. You have a lot to learn… Master.'

'Master!' He straightened his shoulders, 'I like the sound of that. I can't believe you have to pass an exam before your own wand calls you Master.'

'With Zalbar around you're going to have to be on your guard. Zalbar has a way of knowing all that goes on in Sintar. His servants lurk the dark alleyways and unseen spaces of this town.'

'Behind dustbins?' Fizbar asked facetiously.

The voice didn't answer; which was testimony to the stupidity of the question.

Fizbar brushed his nose before replying seriously. 'I know about Zalbar. The streets are filled with fear and unease. It's been like that for years.'

'Which is why you have to be careful as a newly qualified wizard. A wizard of the first order would be a worthy recruit for the Lex Talionis.'

'I'll never join them! NEVER!'

'Not openly, I'm sure. Zalbar has many followers, many we know of, but there are others unknown lurking in the darkness. Some crafty and some with the powers of persuasion.'

Fizbar lifted himself out of his chair. 'You can't trust anyone anymore.' He darted over to the bookcase, popping on his hat as he went.

'We also don't know who their henchmen are. They change so frequently and employ many in different guises,' the voice added.

'I know, I know,' said Fizbar. His head darted back and forth along the shelves. He scratched his forehead whilst pulling out books at random, trying to pinpoint the location of the voice. 'I hate it when I can't see you,' he blurted out with a copy of "Mastering the Effligo Spell" in his hand. He examined the book and remembered mastering the spell with the potions master, Gimera Zelus; he just had no use for it. What could he possibly want to obliterate?

'Try your pocket,' the voice suggested, sighing heavily.

Fizbar positioned the book neatly back in its place and with his other hand dug deep into his pocket. He pulled out a cooking spoon made of ironwood. It was golden in colour with many cherry coils at the spoon's widest point. It looked new and the handle was slightly longer than most similar utensils.

'There you are! I wish you would stop hiding from me like that,' Fizbar complained; then he walked to his desk and sat down. The spoon coughed, as if clearing its throat to speak more clearly. 'I believe you put me there in the first place. I'm a wooden spoon. I don't have any legs or hands, so I can't walk or run anywhere.'

The spoon imagined glancing up at Fizbar's concerned face; at the complete puzzlement in his eyes, and waited intensely for his reply. The wizard furrowed his brow slightly while glancing down at his hand.

'Stop complaining, and making a fuss. Let's not forget you're a wand, so anything's possible!' He tightened his grip, slightly.

'Ouch! A little less grip please.' If the wand had had a

face, tears might have been filling its eyes.

'As long as you know your place.'

'Apparently, in your pocket. Has been for the last few months,' the spoon replied sarcastically. 'It would be nice to see daylight once in a while. More often than just when you need me for spell-casting.'

'That's it. Back in the pocket.' He grabbed the spoon, but stopped as it spoke.

'A little more time please. Your pocket is grubby and stuffy. I can't breathe in there.'

'You're a spoon. You don't need daylight. You've got no eyes and you don't breathe.' Fizbar didn't feel silly talking to a spoon. It's what wizards did; they conversed with their wands. After all, the wands were the wizard's magical guides and conduits of earthly power. Without them wizards could not cast any spells, could not perform any magic, in fact could not be wizards.

'Like you, one can dream…' The spoon sighed heavily. Fizbar walked back to his table and dropped it hard on the tabletop. He picked up a newspaper from a pile in front of him. In an aggrieved tone the spoon said: 'I do have a name you know.'

'I know… Thurrock… But I like spoon better. It's easier on the tongue.' He flicked through the paper, without interest. He closed it and gorped at the front cover. 'I can't believe it! Have you seen this?'

'Remember… No eyes.'

'Hmm!'

The headlines read: *Wizard Thwarts Dragon with Kitchen Utensil.*

'I mean, who thinks up this stuff. Why don't they focus on the fact we're wizards? It's not my fault a spoon picked me. Why can't the headlines read: *Wizard Saves Person from Being Burnt Alive by Lunatic Dragon?*'

'That's too long.'

'You know what I mean.'

'I doubt that.'

Fizbar raised his black eyebrows. 'All right, so I may have conjured up another dragon. But if that first one hadn't been there, the other one wouldn't have fought it, and we wouldn't have gotten rid of the first dragon in the first place!'

'I see.' The spoon clearly didn't.

'I mean, I did the job the Council gave to me. I got rid of the dragon; so a little praise in the media wouldn't have gone amiss. It just makes my job harder. I need good press coverage to launch my career, not this kind of rubbish.'

He tossed the newspaper in the direction of the bin, but it just opened and fanned out all over the floor. He ignored the mess, shook his head and brushed his crimson tunic that was adorned with blue trimmings. His eyes turned towards a clock on his wall as he leant back on his chair. A rush of adrenaline ensued as he glanced at the time. Fizbar launched himself from his seat; then ran towards the door grabbing the handle.

'Forgetting something, Fizbar?' asked the spoon.

Fizbar took off his hat and scratched his head, thinking hard and then realised. 'Oh! Sorry…' He raced back to the table, reached for his wand and popped it into his pocket. He made for the door.

'Again, no sunlight,' the spoon protested in a muffled voice.

'Stop talking.'

'All alone… In the dark… Why me? Why him?'

'That's enough!'

'Where are we going anyway in such a rush?' The spoon was both eager and inquisitive.

'It's a new day and the Council have another job for me.'

This time there was no reply.

4

An Odd Job

'Ah, Fizbar Trundle!' Feltus Stile hailed, 'you've arrived at last!' He was the Council Magistrate. His eyes fixed on Gimera Zelus, the Archmage who was sat among the onlookers and opposite the Council bench.

'Y-Yes,' said Fizbar looking slightly daunted.

'Hmm. Better late than never I suppose. Now we can proceed.' Feltus unrolled a cream parchment and drew it close to his face, millimetres from the tip of his nose. He narrowed his eyes, scanning the document through the small spectacles that rested quaintly at the tip of his long and pointy nose. Fizbar felt uneasy and nervous as he sat in a box at the epicentre of what looked like a courtroom. He glanced over his shoulder at an array of individuals seated behind him on raised benches. Tall men, short men, plump women, small women, students, old wizards, young wizards, chubby wizards and non-wizards; even the odd gnome, and a pixie who sat on his own, which was peculiar given they are usually seen in groups. Fizbar felt as though he were on trial; in the middle of a bullring waiting for the bull's charge. He picked out Gimera from the onlookers. The Archmage sat in a relaxed manner with folded arms. He had a square face, wide forehead and a strong jaw-line that sported a well-oiled goatee. His moustache coiled at each end, but this didn't affect his reserved and impassive presence. He smiled disparagingly at Fizbar through his perfectly straight teeth.

'If I may,' said the plump and red-faced Feltus. 'We have a few pressing matters that need putting right. Looking at today's orders it seems clear to me that Sintar is experiencing a flood of unruly behaviour.' He welcomed the support from the Council members who made low mumblings, nodding their heads with a couple of them throwing in *here here's*. Fizbar raised a hand as if in class; his index finger flexed.

'And before you ask me what troubles I have that need a wizard's intervention, let me tell you, it's malevolence! Irresponsible individuals! I know these are trialling times and that Sintar is not what it used to be thanks to Zalbar and his Lex Talons.' Again, mumblings all around, but this time much louder.

'Lex Talionis,' corrected a frail voice from the Council bench.

'What?'

'It's Lex Talionis, not Lex Talons.'

'Whatever they're called, there will come a day when

normal order is restored. And that's when I can finally retire,' said Feltus, beaming at his Council members who opted to say nothing in response.

Fizbar's hand was still in the air. 'Excuse me.' All eyes on the Council bench shot towards him. 'What does that have to do with me?' he asked, clearly intimidated by the elders.

'What has it got to do with you?' Feltus said raising his voice. 'It's got everything to do with you, and all of us for that matter. Zalbar and his cronies affect everyone in Sintar. And we know he's determined to get his hands on The Grimoire.'

'But…'

'It's thanks to Therolius that we are all still here!'

'But…'

'And Gimera, of course.' Feltus bowed his pumpkin head at the Archmage who reciprocated.

'But—'

'But what, boy? Spit it out!'

'Zalbar hasn't been seen for years; ever since Therolius—'

'Let's not revisit that ordeal again, let it rest. We all know what happened.'

'So why am I here?'

'Haven't you been listening?'

'Attentively.'

'We need to bring order back to our town.'

'I'm not following you,' Fizbar admitted.

'No… You seldom do,' Feltus said with a wry smile. 'Sometimes I forget how little you really *do* know. I'm amazed that you passed your exams, especially with a… Spoon.'

'Are you implying I'm not a wizard?'

'Yes, that's exactly what I am implying. Falzard, yes; wizard, I'm afraid not. If you want an example of a wizard, I suggest you look over there.' He jabbed a finger towards Gimera smiling obsequiously at the Archmage.

'I'm not having this,' said Fizbar getting out of his seat.

'Sit back down!' shouted Feltus, watching as Fizbar complied instantly. 'You could be a blessing just as well as a curse dear boy. I'm just not sure which just yet,' said Feltus with a gentler tone. 'Anyway, getting back to matters at hand. For some strange reason Therolius has urged us to give you another job. We always like to please the School and the Overlord and so the Council decided to accord his request.'

'Therolius suggested me? Why me?' I was never a prize pupil at the school. Generally Therolius was quite dismissive of me.'

'I can't imagine why,' muttered one of the Council members by the name of Lenwick Rile. He was a small, old man with a fixed expression of surprise, as if the wind had changed and left him that way. He had extremely long thin arms, which made him look ill-proportioned.

The Council elders looked blankly at each other in the hope that Feltus would carry on. Their eyes darted everywhere, each muttering random words that were not clear.

A small, pale and elderly, longhaired man took out his false teeth and then spoke. 'Therolius has always been a campaigner for Falzard's. He thinks they are wizards and need to be given their rightful title. It's hard to agree with him, especially seeing as the Lex Talionis are all Falzard's.'

'Except for one!' shouted Fizbar.

Lenwick coughed. 'There is always one bad egg.' He put his teeth back in.

'Thank you, Kellog. I agree with you,' said Feltus. 'Now, getting back to business. What job can we give this boy?'

'Wizard!' said Fizbar annoyed at being called a boy.

'Whatever.' Feltus's head seemed to be shaking. In fact he was reading. 'Oh yes... the old hag Ogeran is in town again. There's a court order that forbids her from setting foot in Sintar.' He raised the parchment in the air, waving it frantically, trying to focus on the words whilst grumbling. 'She is playing up again and needs a good talking to. She's stealing...vegetables, this time using spells, from the garden belonging to...' He paused only for a split-second. 'Kellog West...er...veld!' He raised his head gradually before fixing his gaze on Kellog who sat next to him with a contented smile on his face.

'What say you?' Feltus asked. Kellog shrugged his shoulders. Fizbar hesitated for a fraction of a second, slightly nervous.

'No Kellog. You know very well that Council member grievances are dealt with directly by the Order of Light, the Archmage and his wizards.'

Fizbar remembered being given his first job and the rules that pertained to all such jobs. The Council would receive all grievances from the area. If they were deemed to be of a magical nature then wizards were summoned to deal with them. Every level of wizard was called up, but complaints were delegated to the appropriate levels of competence under the guidance of the Archmage. A wizard would be given four complaints. He had the right to choose only one of them, subject to the Archmage's veto. The council would read the four in sequence. If the wizard chose one and the Archmage opposed it, the next would be read and so forth. Fizbar and his wand listened attentively whilst Feltus read on.

'The next complaint deals with brownies posing as gnomes in the local tavern. The tavern keeper will not serve them until their ID's are confirmed. A wizard is needed to establish their true identities. What say you?'

Fizbar shot from his seat. 'Yes!' He didn't need any time to decide as his wand had shouted out for him. A loud roar came from the crowd as well as the elders.

'Keep your wand under control, boy.'

'It's wizard, not boy!'

'Whatever,' Feltus replied, flapping at him repeatedly, gesturing for him to sit.

Fizbar hissed at his spoon.

'No,' said Zackary Helman getting to his feet. His clothes suited a gentleman and a large gold chain hung from his waistcoat vanishing into his trouser pocket. It flickered bright in some parts as the light hit it. His face was round and his belly plump. His small eyes were hidden behind large spectacles that seemed to make them even smaller, almost pip-like. He explained his opposing view. 'Surely this is a job any wizard can do?'

'Yes, so what's your point?' asked Feltus.

'Well, maybe this job should be given to a newly qualified wizard.'

'But Fizbar is relatively new and qualified,' Feltus countered.

'Yes, but maybe this could be given to a very fresh graduate. It's a basic task. Why even an apprentice could do this; a tenderfoot!' Voices rose again filling the room. Feltus looked at Gimera for advice. Fizbar sat in silence, his eyes waiting. They needed the Archmage's consent for the objection to be upheld. Gimera nodded. Fizbar slumped in his seat, disappointed, and felt a twitch in his neck.

'Order!' Feltus banged a hammer on the desk. The

voices eventually died down. 'Well then, moving on; a dragon and...' He cut himself short. 'No. Clearly you've already had an experience with a dragon.' He looked at Gimera who shook his head in an irritated manner. Clearly he agreed with Feltus. This was now the fourth and final complaint.

Feltus scanned the document turning it over, but the other side was blank. 'Which leaves only the last one,' he announced.

Suddenly a tall, thin lady walked into the courtroom holding a small piece of paper. She placed it in front of Feltus and whispered in his ear. He looked at Fizbar with a deceitfully civil grin. Feltus cleared his throat as the lady left the room.

'Another case has come to our attention. There is a problem with a hunchback in Filtzer Forest.' He read the paper carefully before putting it down. 'It seems some little sprites are giving this hunchback a hard time. It appears they have somehow cured his twin of his hump, but haven't done the same for him, so he's caged them all up and is threatening to eat them. Don't know much more I'm afraid, but I feel this is the one for you, Fizbar.' His eyes ran up and down the Council bench, but he had already decided for them. 'Should be simple enough for your...' He cleared his throat. 'Level.' He looked over to Gimera who tilted his head in agreement. Fizbar didn't want to cause a scene with a counter-rule, which would mean having to list a plausible reason why he didn't want the job. A dislike for hunchbacks wasn't enough to support an objection. He put a hand into his pocket turning his wand and fidgeting.

'Err… I guess so,' he said quietly.

'Is that a yes, Trundle? Please state it for the Council. Speak up boy.'

'Yes, I'll…take the job, and my correct title is wizard.'

The Council immediately rose and made their way to the door. In fact everybody in the Council chamber got up at the same time. The movement in the room was fast. The chatter heightened behind Fizbar who was still in the box feeling sorry for himself. He looked at the Archmage who leisurely lifted himself off the bench, smiling. He sensed venom in Fizbar's gaze, but couldn't for the life of him understand why. Maybe he was reading something that wasn't there. The noise in the room rose to a new level. The Council secretary, Maxine Drool, was the only seated individual, typing away on her stenotype; talking to herself, heedless of the surrounding racket.

Fizbar pulled out his wand and looked at it. 'Horrible case. I don't know if I can do this.'

'Of course you can,' said his wand. 'I wouldn't say it's all bad. Filtzer Forest is not a lovely place, but at least it's always dimly lit. They say the little sprites have kept it that way since the uprising.'

'Korrigans. They're little pests. I don't like them either.'

'Whether you like hunchbacks or not Fizbar, this inquiry involves one and there's no escaping it if you want to advance.'

'I know. It wouldn't be bad if it were during the day though. I don't like the dark either.'

Fizbar's wand shouted in a muffled voice as he popped it into his pocket.

'*I know the feeling!*'

5

A Familiar Place

'ONCE upon a time, long… Very long ago, in the midst of Sintar stood a gloomy forest, so large that it would take many, many days to walk across it. It was an enchanted forest, for all night it was the haunt of the little people in the neighbourhood. They would skip and dance all night long and far into the next day, but the moment the midday sun streamed down upon them, they would all run away leaving rings on the grass to mark the place of their nightly revels—'

'All right, that's enough storytelling!'

'I haven't finished yet.'

'Yes, you have.'

'You don't appreciate good tales do you?'

'Good tales, yes. Your stories, no.'

There was silence.

'Fizbar.'

'What?'

'Can I call you Fizz?'

'No.'

'Why not?'

'Because it's not my name.'

'I know. I'm just trying to be modern; to fit in.'

'You don't need to fit in. It's me that needs to fit in.'

'You're a wizard, Fizbar. Don't let the word Falzard play on your mind. That name's just been created by the elitists to mock us.'

'What do you mean us?'

'You know, all the lesser wizards as well as us – your guides.'

'But I *am* a wizard.'

'Maybe I used the wrong word. How about inferior?'

'You're digging a deeper hole.'

'Or—'

'Shall we just continue?' Fizbar cut the spoon short.

'I'd also prefer you to use my name properly.'

'Thurrock?'

'Correct!'

'But spoon is simpler, and easier.'

'Why is that?' The spoon was blunt.

'Because you *are* a spoon.'

There was no response this time. The spoon was either tight-lipped or sulking.

Fizbar panted a few times whilst climbing a long and winding road. He was huffing and puffing and his feet felt warm, heavy and sore. His breath was laboured like someone who had never exercised. The loud breathing was annoying his wand. After an hour they had reached the brim of the forest. Still out of breath, Fizbar mustered his last few available gasps to form words.

'Finally… We're here!' He then swallowed hard, wincing as the saliva scraped his dry and tender throat.

'I don't want to sound smarmy,' said the spoon.

'That would be a change!' replied Fizbar before the spoon could finish.

'Fizbar?'

'Yes?' Fizbar had both hands on his hips. His breathing was gradually returning to normal.

'Why didn't you just use your wand to get here? It would have saved time.'

Fizbar bit his lip feeling stupid. The wand was right, Fizbar could have used it to travel; in a puff of smoke, or a whizz of his wand, he could have been at the forest in no time at all. Thinking hard for a reason he finally replied. 'I needed the exercise. Just look at me. Just listen to my breathing!' He felt even more stupid.

'But you're as thin as a rake!'

'Doesn't mean I don't need the exercise.'

'It's beyond me. We've been practising the *itio* spell for a while now. Besides…'

'Besides, how do you know I'm thin if you can't see? One of these days I'm going to buy you stick-on eyes!'

His wand huffed. 'I wish you'd stop saying things like

that. I can see with my "magic" eyes. You really know how to dampen a spoon's spirit don't you?'

The wizard turned a deaf ear and looking up at the row of towering trees, he relaxed. He took a deep breath, and then strode forwards looking around cautiously. The spooky glade ahead was quiet. His wand arm was relaxed, but his wand was pointing forwards into the dark of the night. A sudden murder of crows and jackdaws rushed upwards startling him vanishing into the trees, cawing and squeaking. He swallowed hard. He didn't feel comfortable here. He didn't like it. As he continued to walk he glanced back at the entrance, which was now well in the distance. Fizbar hadn't realised how far he had already walked, but he knew he had almost arrived and there was no going back. A faint, ghostly mist slowly manifested from the ground. It was unique to this forest and people told stories about its cruel games of misleading you in strange directions. Only crazy people would consider occupying or even entering Filtzer Forest; however there had been quite a few of them over the years. Fizbar didn't feel welcome. His wand was quiet, too quiet. He knew a large lake was ahead with tall, dark and dead trees surrounding it. That's what people said. That's what the maps showed. That's what he had learnt at school. Sintarian stories were sometimes an exaggeration, but Fizbar felt that most were genuine and based on real events. He knew the history of the forest, but didn't allow that to deter him. He had a job to do and he focused on that.

'No wonder very few people have come here,' said Fizbar.

'Mostly elite wizards as they have the power to ward off any malevolence.'

'It depends on what kind of evil haunts this place.'

'Are you referring to Zalbar?' asked the spoon.

'Him and his cronies. Also those for hire and who have no scruples or virtue.'

'Only the hunchbacks are brave enough to enter here.'

'Mad enough you mean,' said Fizbar, and then hesitating slightly, he added, 'then it's wizards like us that have to bail them out.'

'I suppose. It is strange that the Council haven't had any hunchback jobs since...'

'Yes... I know.'

His wand sent an unhurried shock along his arm and up towards his neck until it tickled the top of his head. It made his hairs stand on end. The spoon felt something and it translated into sketchy bright visions that flashed in Fizbar's mind. He looked around, still treading lightly on the forest floor even though his head was starting to tingle. He began to have visions of terrible faces, expressions and even feelings of pain. He closed his eyes to black out the visions, and then stopped. He unconsciously opened his hand and time seemed to slow down as he dropped his wand. When it hit the ground everything seemed to revert to normality. The visions left as quickly as they had come, but it felt like an eternity to Fizbar. He bent over, picked up his wand and despite a familiar feeling he carried on walking.

'Did you... Feel that?' asked Fizbar in a leery voice.

There was no answer. They had arrived at the lake. It was the specially favoured spot with all the little people. Fizbar noticed something in the distance and continued to walk towards it, still wondering what had just happened. After a short walk along a stony path bordered with rocks, a passage opened up to him as if a curtain had been lifted. The stones gave way to a muddy path that spiralled into a small cave-like entrance.

'I bet that's where the hunchback has his captives.'

Fizbar had already begun examining his surroundings, looking for clues. His head was a little sore but he managed to ignore it to focus on the job at hand.

'Why's that?' The spoon enquired.

Fizbar pointed to the floor. 'See that green goo? That's hunchback saliva and it leads the way.'

'Are you sure? How do you know the hunchback is even in there?'

'Hunchbacks don't like people.'

'And they've hated wizards ever since the subversion,' the spoon added.

Fizbar scanned his surroundings. 'I know. Ever since they rebelled against us. From placid public servants to angry combatants.'

'They weren't servants.' The wand spat, if such a thing were was possible. It felt distressed by the statement.

'Well, they didn't like wizards for a strange reason. I'm not surprised that nobody talks about it anymore.' He found the entrance. 'Hmm. I just don't know how I'm going to do this,' said Fizbar. He thought hard about turning back. He really didn't like hunchbacks, but he had made it this far and the thought of becoming a Wizard of the Second Order gave him the extra drive.

'Okay. Let's go.' He grabbed his wand firmly and raised both hands until his arms formed an arch. He mirrored this action with his legs and his feet pointed in opposite directions. It was an odd sight.

'I sense you're doing something extremely bizarre,' the spoon commented.

'For your information this is the "wizarding stance"; all wizards do this. It tells others we're to be reckoned with.' He was happy and firm with his answer, even though he looked like an hourglass and moved like a drunken ballerina.

'All I know is that I wish I wasn't your wand.'

Fizbar made his way slowly through the underground passage keeping his stance. A minute passed.

'We could also have tried the *peragro* spell for "wandering through" or *percursatio* for "travelling through" or—'

'Taceo.' Fizbar cut the wand short.

'…No, that spell's for muting or when you want someone to sh—Oh, I see. Well you'll see in the future. I just hope nothing horrid happens!'

'I'm just saying…'

'And I'm just saying that I'm your magical guide; it's my duty to improve your magical ability. How can I help if you don't take me seriously? The Grimoire doesn't teach you everything, you know,' the wand spouted in a burst of ill temper.

'The Grimoire does.'

'Doesn't.'

'Does.'

'I'm not going to argue with you, Fizbar.'

'Why don't we just focus on the task at hand?'

Fizbar hit his head upon the low entrance, failing to squat as he moved under the low turf-roof. His hat was knocked to the floor. He bent over, picked it up and popped it back onto his now sore forehead. He rubbed it hard a few times until the pain lightened. He grimaced as he ran a hand over the affected area. After a few seconds he managed to resume his stance. The wand tutted, but certainly not out of sympathy. He walked a couple of paces bent slightly and forced his wand arm out firm and fully extended.

'*You first*,' Fizbar instructed the wand, but as he did, he stumbled on a bump on the ground and they both toppled down a slimy slide, which led deeper into the cave. The wand wailed and Fizbar mewled as they rolled down a steep slide emitting a series of shrieks and cries as they went. Finally Fizbar slid into a large and slimy pool of green gloop.

'That was a spot of luck,' the wand said happily.

'What do you mean? I'm covered in this horrible sticky green—' His nose upturned at the strong smell. 'And revolting…'

'Well, lucky me then. I seem to have landed somewhere less vile.'

Fizbar's eyes darted here and there. He found his wand sitting on a pile of dirty grey linen that appeared to have started out as white sheets, which now looked like they hadn't been washed in decades. They also had tears, holes and poor attempts at repairing with gaudy patchwork. A pillow and a sack added to the heap.

The cave was hollow, dark, dank and very, very smelly. Cold water dripped from the stone crevices trickling down the limestone walls. A thin waft of breeze blew down the slide they had fallen down. The wizard hauled himself out of the sticky substance. His cloak was now several times its original weight and with heavy steps he managed to trudge over and pick up his wand.

The wand let out a tiny squeal, as if it could feel a chill from the gooey touch of his master. He was only humouring Fizbar. '*Lighten up,*' whispered the wand.

'*No. I don't want to raise any suspicion,*' said Fizbar.

'*Detergeo!*' He forced a whisper, pointing his wand directly the pile of dirty linen and golden sparkles appeared around the heap. The other hit a stalactite at his leather boots. A yellow spark hit the floor, and then split into two, before bouncing in opposing directions and dancing like two angry glow-worms. One of the sparks landed on unhinging it from the roof. It hit it again. Then again; this time breaking it. As it fell, Fizbar looked up, and in a startled manner leapt forwards, only to slip and fall onto the pile of sparkles that engulfed him in a golden sheet of flickering light. He looked at his hands and the green slime began to shrink until it vanished and he was left clean. So was the pile of linen. Immaculately clean. He lifted himself out of the heap and brushed his attire a couple of times, causing tiny billows of dust around his hands. His wand coughed. Fizbar sneezed.

'What did you say about not raising suspicion?'

'There! That's much better.' Fizbar was satisfied.

The wand grunted, as if unamused by the event and Fizbar's carelessness. The wizard squinted into the dark ahead and walked a couple of paces, both arms extended whilst taking baby steps.

'All right then.' He lifted his wand. '*Ilumino.*' Suddenly his wand lit up completely, a powerful glow radiated from the tip of the spoon.

'Great... Now I feel like I'm on a sunbed,' said the

wand with a bitter edge.

'*Shhh! It's dark down there and I hate the dark!*' Fizbar whispered. His heart started to thump faster. He could hear it even above his loud breathing. They continued further down the trail, along a dip in the path. Odd drips of water landed and splashed on the puddles of the uneven floor, breaking the silence. They ventured further down the path until all you could see was the glow of white light from the spoon. Fizbar hit his head again on another low ridge, but this time his hat didn't fall off. He walked a little further until a speck of orange light became visible. He looked above and around as he continued, rubbing his head. He noticed he was walking down a large and tubular cavity, then down what seemed like huge stairs. It was lined with a transparent substance that looked like ice. It seemed to be a glacial cave; it was certainly cold enough. The light from his wand suddenly vanished.

'*What's happened? Where's the light?*' asked Fizbar.

'*You cast the spell not me. Maybe if you had been firmer in your tone the light would have lasted longer, after all you did say it like a fairy.*'

'*Well I couldn't exactly shout it out. Someone might have heard me!*' Fizbar replied.

'*Well if you—*'

'*Shhh!*' Fizbar had heard something.

'*What is it?*'

'*I heard something.*'

There was a short pause, and then clanks and groans emerged faintly from the distance.

'*I heard it too!*' said the wand in a hushed tone. '*What was it? The hunchback?*'

'*I see something.*'

'*Where?*'

'*There! The light.*' The wizard pointed ahead into the pitch black.

'*Well... I believe you are pointing, which again—*'

'*Okay, no eyes. How is it that you can hear and not see?*'

'*I don't know. Sometimes I even surprise myself,*' said the wand.

6

A Badger in the Alley

The evening was warm and dusk was minutes away. The storm clouds overhead were waiting to set free yet another downpour over Sintar. Therolius peered up into the blackness as he locked the front door of the school building. Feeling tired and hungry he set off home. The streets were wet and quiet, but people were still passing by; acknowledging the Overlord along his usual route home. Some had umbrellas covering their faces; others newspapers preventing the fine misty spray that filled the air from wetting them. The pavement was slippery, but Therolius managed to walk along an uneven cobbled street without slipping until it met an alley. It was tight and only two people side-by-side could manage to squeeze through it; but it was as a shortcut Therolius often took. After a few paces the restricting passageway began to widen. It was still narrow, but became a tight backstreet, which eventually led into the main street. Passing BFF (Best Friend's Forever) a shop that sold basic staffs for fifth level wizards, he glanced through the window, thinking he needed another one. A warm smile beamed from his wet-haired face. The wind sneaked up from behind him, so he drew his cloak tighter around himself. On the other side of the alley was *A Magical Craft*, the wand maker. In the window was a small section with the label *Falzard must haves, 50% discounts* mounted on a chopping board, which was the centrepiece of the sale. He let out a little chesty cough, which was meant to be a laugh of disagreement. He wrapped himself a little more tightly fastening the toggles on his cloak and pulled his hat down firmly as the wind started to lift it. The alley was quiet except for the whistling wind. There was nobody in sight.

Therolius arrived at a wider section of the alley, which allowed more of the wind to gust through. He passed some metal dustbins and shook his head at all the waste that had built up. Bits of food were scattered over the ground; the dustbins were all full and overflowing with their lids floating on top of the trash. One of the lids slipped off its tower of rubbish and fell to the ground. The sudden clatter made Therolius jump. A cat darted off meowing as it sped around a corner. He felt a panicky rush of blood, followed by a faint chill crawling up his spine. It was generally safe to walk alone at night, especially if you were a wizard. Even more so as Overlord, but tonight there was something else in the air. The wind felt dryer than usual, almost restricting and somehow wrong for a wet night. He surveyed the area with closer attention than usual. The sprays of water had settled and the air was clear, but residues of black smoke became visible to his left; close to him. Then a gust of wind thrust his hat to one side as something whooshed past him on his right. Again bits of black smoke dangled, and then dissipated quickly before he could focus on them. He raised his brow and his small glasses slipped down the bridge of his nose. With an index finger Therolius pushed them back up; and as he did this, his cloak opened and the breeze fanned it like a peacock. He dipped his hand into his pocket finding solace and security in his faithful wand.

'I know you are here. The evidence is visible,' said Therolius as he picked up on lingering strands of the black smoke.

'Just waiting for you to greet me old man,' said a ghostly voice as it echoed from various points in the alleyway. A few seconds later a black smokey figure in the shape of a man emerged facing Therolius. Black smokey strips twirled and meshed together and the form was unmistakable.

'Viktor Witfar.' Therolius identified the figure without hesitation; even before he had fully formed, 'I knew it wouldn't be long before Zalbar recruited you to the Lex Talionis. I'm actually surprised it took this long.'

'The Badger, if you please… Overlord.' Viktor insisted as his form finally turned to a solid physical state. 'I didn't need convincing; it was a cause I felt strongly about.'

His eye patch exemplified his washed-up pirate demeanour. A streak of white hair ran down the centre of his wiry black hair; the distinctive feature that had given rise to the name "The Badger". His clothes were black and tattered; he looked more like a beggar. He smiled showing his dirty and stained teeth. His breath matched their appearance and was complemented by bloodless, weathered and leathery skin. Viktor paced aimlessly curling his wiry hair with his dirty fingers. His hands were wrapped in unclean and tattered linen. He took a deep breath and said, 'I have a lot of skills to offer his Lordship.' Viktor flickered into a smokey black cloud, and then back again to his physical form; his eye patch was the only item that didn't vanish.

'That I *can* believe, but only my dear friends and family call me Therolius.'

Viktor made a face. 'Forget propriety old man, all that is nonsensical!' He waved his hand as if clearing the air of his words. 'I know you have what Lord Zalbar wants, so it would be much, much easier if you handed it over to me. Save your old bones the stress of battle.'

Viktor reached out, turning his hand a couple of times until his palm pleaded with the Overlord. His fingers moved, gesturing Therolius to hand over what he required. His head bobbed up and down, in a hurried motion.

'I am terribly sorry badger, tortoise or whatever alias

you use, but I have no idea what you are talking about,' said Therolius firmly and with a hint of ridicule. The Badger stared at him with evil intent.

'If you are referring to "The Grimoire" you can tell Zalbar to come and get it himself.' He knew that wasn't what Viktor wanted. 'He tried it once, but we all know what happened on that occasion.' Therolius raised his eyebrows, softly cleared his throat and raised his wand in a spiralling motion. 'Let him try again.'

The Badger's good eye focused on the tip of the Overlord's wand. 'Forget it old man, your magic will not work on me.' He surveyed Therolius, and began flickering at intervals between smoke and his human form. 'I have my mother to thank for that,' he said in a bitter voice.

'Your mother was a smoke demon, and a nasty piece of work. It seems you've inherited her traits. It was a pity your father's good nature was weaker than hers. Instead, they created an abomination – you! I am so sorry you turned out like this, Viktor.'

The Badger's flickering became rapid, his tone elevated. He became flustered, and then he growled.

'I don't want your pity old man. I want that journal. Now give it to me or I will make you wish you were never born.' Viktor pointed as the tattered linen hung loosely from his arm like mummified bandages. Therolius stood firm, with his wand ready for action.

'Zalbar will not get anything from me. Sending his

lackey is but another failed tactic which show's weakness.'

'You really think so?' Viktor hissed at the Overlord, 'then we will have to give you a little something to make you reconsider.' The Badger dipped a hand into his pocket, brought out a crow's feather, and slowly raised it until it met the Overlord's eyes. Therolius knew Viktor's intention was to dispose of him. He was surprised that Zalbar had not confronted him himself, and now he knew why.

'Lord Zalbar has shown you how to channel your father's energy.'

'Yes. A smoke demon with a wand, now isn't that frightening?'

'Do you honestly think a *Falzard* can defeat the Overlord?' Therolius didn't like the reference. He hated the labelling, but in this case it was to his advantage to use it.

'Do you think I'm stupid? I know the great Therolius Delrunt despises that association. We all know about your campaign to unite all wizards, whatever their wands may be and to rid Sintar of what you call "magical bullying".'

Viktor spat on the ground before continuing:

'To answer your impending question, yes, I am competent enough to confront you.'

'Bullying you say? It appears you practice what you preach; quite literally,' said Therolius, whilst surveying the area, and getting his bearings.

'Zalbar is the evil player here, Viktor.'

'That's funny. Zalbar told me the exact same thing about you.' He pretended to cry, wiping away imaginary tears from his eyes. 'You don't think that I should be treated as a wizard?'

'*Certainly not!*' Therolius replied firmly.

Viktor raised his feather until his arm was fully extended. Therolius responded with the same movements, aiming high.

'In that case I won't delay with idle chat. Maybe my friends will encourage you to reconsider.' Viktor took a few steps backwards, creating a larger space between them. 'I want that journal! And I'm going to get it, whatever it takes!' He flicked his wand, pointing at the wizard's body and spoke through clenched teeth. '*Reformidatio.*'

A swarm of flies appeared in front of Viktor. Then it gradually formed into six little people with medieval-looking metal hats. Their extremely long thin ears became visible, with tufts of hair poking out from each end. Black hair shot from their tightly fitted hats and fell short of their shoulders. They were half the size of the Overlord and resembled skinny gnomes. Their bodies were bare, but from the waist down to their feet brown hair covered their skin. Their eyes were narrow, raised and slanted; their pouted mouths were wide and their teeth matched Viktor's. They moved forwards slowly, growling, trying to circle the Overlord, forcing him back and towards the dustbins. Viktor clapped his hands in anticipation, enjoying the moment; now with his feather behind his ear. The Overlord stepped backwards three paces and the little people moved forward.

'I hate kobolds!' said Therolius as he lifted his wand ready to cast a spell.

One of the kobolds struck first, running speedily towards him, savage-like. Therolius pointed his wand at the creature. '*Cremo conflo!*'

For a moment it seemed as though nothing had happened. Then the kobold let out an echoing screech before bursting into flames. The remaining kobolds looked at each other with their fiendish yellow eyes and barked ferociously. Two bloodthirsty kobolds ran up and leapt from the alley walls, flanking the Overlord. His eyes darted from left to right and his wand's movement failed to keep up. The kobold on the left scampered at the wizard, but he had already cast the spell and it burst into flames. Seconds later the other kobold ran further up the wall and dived at Therolius like a cat leaping on his prey. He could not swing his wand round in time. The kobold's face was inches away from the Overlord as it struck him and knocked him over flat on his back. His wand went flying and landed close by; next to a dustbin. The vicious creature attempted to bite at the Overlord, managing to rip his cloak. It frowned. It took a piece of linen, growled like a rabid dog and tried spitting it out. The linen was caught between its razor-like teeth. Therolius stretched his left arm out, managing to wriggle out of his cloak. He couldn't see his wand and he was still pinned down by the kobold. He noticed the dustbin lid a few feet from his hand and then saw his wand. He stretched out his wand arm, stretching so hard it felt as though his arm would pop from its socket. The wand was still inches away from his hand. The linen flew from the kobold's mouth and just before he could take another bite Therolius grabbed the lid and swung it round hitting the creature flat in the face, forcing it off him. It sat shaking its head. Therolius grabbed his wand and cast the spell whilst kneeling. '*Stinguo!*' The kobold burst into dust, but this caused four more to run towards him, one of them jumping up high. The Overlord shouted '*Centoquadonis!*' This time four strands of fiery light shot from his wand. Quicker than before and they all burst into flames, and the ashes fell, covering him and the ground.

Viktor conjured up another four, annoyed at the Overlord's resistance. The remaining four regrouped and ran together towards Therolius. He could not direct a single spell at all four of them and he had to think quickly. Suddenly, as the kobolds were inches from him he held his wand with both hands and pointing it upwards he shouted, '*Testudo conflo!*' Radiance encased the Overlord and as the kobolds hit the light, they burst into flames. Ashes fell again and his wand was already pointing in the direction of Viktor. He looked around but The Badger was nowhere in sight. All that remained were black smokey strands in the air. Viktor was gone.

'You can tell Zalbar that he should do his own dirty work instead of sending an amateur,' Therolius shouted, whilst regaining his breath. The shield flickered and then fizzled out. He looked down at the wet ground covered in ash, his hands on his knees. He kicked some of the ash that had turned to mush. Therolius realised that circumstances had changed and matters would only worsen. Zalbar's plans were reaching further afield; his group was becoming more powerful. He was equipping the Lex Talionis with magic. Eventually, Zalbar would send more of the Lex Talionis for the journal he so deeply wanted. Therolius knew he had to think of a safe place for the journal. He thought hard on the way home about a place nobody would suspect. Before long he knew what he had to do. The evening became very humid and the night had settled in. The air now smelt like a barbecue.

7

Korrigans

The warm light grew as Fizbar walked closer, trying to make out the source of a deep muffled voice. It grew louder with each step. Then he heard little prattles that became louder as he drew near; then their pitches climbed. He entered a warmly lit chamber and managed to keep himself hidden behind a group of stalagmites that had formed into a shape very much like a hand. Treading carefully he stepped on the slippery surface and positioned himself between the stalagmites, peering through the gap as he fixed his eyes on the commotion ahead. A large hunchback paced around, surrounded by torches. He shuffled and sniffled, circling a huge bird-like cage that was suspended from the cave ceiling. The chain from the top of the cage seemed to vanish into the blackness above, as the cave was large. The hunchback was broad and dressed in filthy green clothes. Fizbar upturned his nose, as a whiff of what could only be hunchback odour travelled his way. The hunchback had little hair on a head that looked like a giant and slightly squashed potato. His eyes were not even, the left veered off to the left, the other looking right. For a moment the hunchback peered behind him, his ears flapped like small pancakes, and his lopsided mouth revealed tooth decay and thick drooling saliva. His hunch was large and deformed. He must have found it difficult to cloth himself, especially as his deformity extended to his clubbed right foot that dragged on the floor as he moved.

'YOU LIED! Humpy, Hunchy, Humpy, Hunchy. Make it go AWAY!' said the hunchback, both harrowed and vexed. His deep bland voice sounded toneless and flat, but his last words appeared somewhat sincere. There was almost a hint of sadness in his words.

Three little creatures rattled the cage, like wild ferrets. They looked like pygmy trolls, but were even smaller. Even smaller than gnomes with their large floppy triangular ears. Each ear was as big as their head. 'Get us out of here you Lump! Lump! Lump!'

'Yes, let us out you big ugly swelling! You walnut! You twit!'

'Oh look!' one of them pointed at the hunchback. 'There's a giant slug on your shoulder and it's going to eat your leg!' They all laughed in unison and in annoying pitches.

Fizbar shook his head. The little people, were supposed to look enchanting and act in a friendly not fiendly manner.

'They're ugly little things aren't they? Where are their

little pink ballerina dresses and sweet chants?' whispered Fizbar to his wand.

'What you are seeing is their ugly side. They're annoyed. That's what they become.'

'Become?'

'Yes. They're Korrigans now, like tiny goblins and once they change there's no going back.'

'There must be a way?'

'Wizards have tried to restore their true nature, to turn them back into fairies.'

'How?'

'They need to be in a sealed room filled with sweet things, being told sweets things by sweet people, being given sweet things.'

'Has it worked?'

'I don't think so. Where would you find such things?'

The vision of them holding hands and twirling round, singing rhymes and throwing petals gracefully into the air was far from the present reality. They looked different for starters. Fizbar stared at each of them as their expressions changed. They growled heavily revealing fine rows of sharp teeth; snarling and snapping at the cage following the hunchback as he moved.

'Humpy, Hunchy, Humpy, Hunchy.' The hunchback repeated whilst shuffling round without direction or purpose and almost in tears.

Fizbar felt saddened by the event he was witnessing.

'It was your fault, Lumpy! Your fault, Hunchy Lumpy!' said one of the creatures, whilst the other two whizzed around the cage laughing like madmen.

'Not my fault. Not my fault! I was tired!' The hunchback disagreed whilst bits of the stringy saliva fell to the ground.

Fizbar was leaning hard on a stalagmite; it was beginning to break. He didn't notice. The hunchback shuffled over to the cage and grabbed both sides with his thick hands. The little people began biting savagely at the hunchback's fingers, which made him twist the cage sending it in a spin, as he shouted in pain. He inspected his fingers, making sure they were all still there. The creatures inside rattled madly like wild animals.

'Korrigans?' said Fizbar directing his question to his wand. 'What are they doing here?'

'Guess we are here to find out. Seems they've upset him,' the wand replied, 'of all the creatures to pick on, they chose a hunchback.'

'Don't hunchbacks possess some magical abilities?' asked Fizbar. There was a nervous edge in his voice.

'Hunchbacks? No, but that doesn't mean they are as stupid as people assume. They're not harmless either; they are just as strong as giants.'

'What about the Korrigans? Wouldn't they have fairy-like powers?' the wizard quizzed his wand.

'They do possess some kind of magic, but it's a little trickier.'

'What do you mean?'

'Well their magic is more of an accord, an agreement. They ask for something and have to give something in return. Their magic is nothing more than that, but mischievous all the same.'

'So what do we do?'

'That's not for me to decide, Master,' the wand said hastily. 'You're the wizard!'

'Right, blast them to bits then!'

'Don't forget they're cunning, so be careful. And—'

'What!'

'Don't forget the hunchback. Wizards are not at the top of their list of friends.'

Fizbar continued looking on. The stalagmite continued to break away, slowly, but the wizard had no inkling.

'Let's see how ya like this then,' the hunchback growled as he picked up a torch. The wooden stick was thick and long and a reddish-orange flame burned at the tip. He shuffled gradually over to the cage, dragging his leg. Under it was a neat pile of twigs and fresh peat. He lowered the torch in order to light it. 'Now let's see who's laughing.'

'Do that and your hump will grow even bigger, so big that even your twin brother won't be able to look you in the eye,' said one of the Korrigans through a long pout.

'Yes, you didn't dance for us,' said another.

'Or do any somersaults like you promised,' the other

finished.

Fizbar nodded his head thinking it impossible for a hunchback to perform any acrobats with a hump that size, let alone a somersault. It was silly but the Korrigans were cunning little beings. He thought hard about what to do.

'You didn't give me time to rest!' the hunchback protested. 'I ran to the enchanted glade. Ran to rid this hump, just like ma brother did. I was so afraid of being late I ran and ran as fast as I could to reach you before sunset. I was out of breath and so tired. I could run no more. It hurt. When I reached you, you were dancing and singing so happily. I thought it was done.'

'So what happened? Hmm?' said a Korrigan.

'Yes, what happened?' asked the other.

'I could neither sing nor dance. I tried. I had no breath left for any caper. No energy for a somersault. I've never done a somersault. I don't know what it is.'

The hunchback's brow looked like a rolled up curtain exposing his melon-sized eyes.

'Your brother did. Are you not twins? Can't you do the things he did?' asked a Korrigan with bitterness in his voice.

'You still displeased us. Very much. All we wanted from you was a song and dance. To make us laugh! Was that so difficult? Huh?' said the other.

'Yes, happy, happy. You make us happy and we make you happy. Happy happy!' said another.

'Yes, that's the deal!' The first Korrigan concluded. They looked at each other; then their smiles turned into three differently pitched laughs.

'I tried to do the special dance and sang *Humpty Humpty! Humpty Humpty!* But I was so tired, got so confused and giddy from turning round so fast. Ma hump doesn't allow me to move so fast.' The hunchback sat on a long rock that acted as a bench; resting his large feet. His toes poked through the ends of his boots. He was still holding the torch.

'But instead of singing "Humpty Hunchy Humpty Hunchy" you sang, "Humpty Hunchy sat on the wall" and kept repeating it. That was so annoying,' said a Korrigan with both hands wrapped around the cage bars.

'Yeah! And not very funny!' said another.

'Yes, you even said *sat on wall, sat on wall!* Time and time again!' the other Korrigan added with its long, thin fingers poking from the cage. The Korrigan pressed its face up against the bars reaffirming its grip and spoke slowly. 'Yes, that annoyed us, made our skin crawl. Turned us into Korrigans. So when we took the lake water out of our special flask and poured it over your back, instead of singing *Go away, ugly hump!* We sang *Hump, turn to a lump!* and behold it did!' The Korrigan left the bars and joined the others. They all broke into an array of laughter. The hunchback could feel the terrible weight of the enlarged hump.

'And it's still growing!' said one of the tiny troll-like people. They laughed so loud and hard that for a moment it appeared as though they had lost their breath. The hunchback pulled a hand up to cover his ears. He felt the movement of his hunch. Then suddenly, it grew until it was two times its normal size.

'It will get so heavy that you'll have to crawl on your hands and knees all the way home,' said what appeared to be the chief Korrigan.

'Make it go away… Make it go away,' the hunchback pleaded, even more distressed than before.

'Only a wizard can cure you and we all know what happened between hunchbacks and wizards, long, long ago.' The laughter died a little.

The hunchback managed to lift himself off the bench using most of his strength. He yelled at the pain and weight in his shoulders. Fizbar was open mouthed and shocked by the hunchback's suffering and pulled in disgust hard on the stalagmite. It was then that is broke off with a loud crunch and he fell forward, sliding down another slimy, wet slope arms outstretched until he stopped just paces from the hunchback's large feet. He looked up, startled, and scared.

'Hello,' said Fizbar nervously, yet with a large smile on his face. A big hand pulled him up managing to throw him onto the bench. The Korrigans sucked in air in amazement almost simultaneously, like triplets.

'A wizard? Here?' said a Korrigan.

'I never knew my powers were that strong,' said the chief Korrigan whilst looking at his hands, turning them, amazed at their power. He looked at the others who just burst into laughter.

The hunchback turned to face the wizard. One of his large eyes rolled up and down. There was only one thing on his mind.

'GET RID OF THIS NOW!' growled the hunchback, saliva dripping from his lower jaw, and almost touching the floor like an unmanned bungee.

Fizbar shuffled his hands. He could sense determination in the hunchback's eyes, and his intention of using the large torch he carried. The stench was bad; it appeared the hunchback hadn't washed for a very long time, if ever at all.

'I don't know how,' said Fizbar automatically and honestly.

The hunchback whacked him lightly on the back of his head. He fell off the bench and onto the floor. His hat flew off and to one side. He managed to get up and regain his posture.

'Do it! Or next time you won't get up so easily,' the hunchback warned him.

The Korrigans rattled the cage like chimpanzees, laughing, but cowering at the sight of the wizard. They didn't know Fizbar, but feared what he stood for. He pointed the wand at the cage and paused. The Korrigans looked at each other in fright before they focused on the wand.

'A spoon?' said one of them before they returned to their cackling.

'Not at them! Ma hump! Stop it from growing!' The hunchback was firm and his anger surfaced like a demon. 'NOW!'

'You'd better do something quick Fizbar before his pain turns from words to actions,' his wand suggested.

Fizbar was at a loss. He was confused and didn't know what spell to cast and how to resolve the situation without being hurt. He had only been out of school for three months and now felt the pressure of being a wizard. He didn't like the feeling, but managed to shake it off and turn his attention to the job at hard.

'You can do this Fizbar. You're a wizard,' he muttered to himself.

The hunchback was pacing madly and the Korrigans emitted both laughter and cries. His mind was blank, until suddenly a suitable spell surfaced. As he was about to raise his wand a word left his lips, '*Ablegatio!*'

A vacuum of air was sucked into the chamber extinguishing some of the torches, but not all. Nothing else happened. The hunchback looked up and around. So did the Korrigans. Fizbar shook his wand furiously as if it were broken, then thumped it a couple of times, wondering why nothing was coming out. He turned the spoon until the tip was facing his eye. There was a moment's silence before the Korrigans began to ridicule and point at him. The laughter was so annoying the hunchback turned with a sour look on his face and focused on the wizard. Fizbar managed a half smile whilst shrugging his shoulders.

'What kind of a wizard are you then?' said the hunchback.

'Yes, what kind? Please don't point that spoon at me again, I may have to cook with it!' said a Korrigan in disdain before joining in with the others, sneering and giggling.

'Yes, I may even wet my pants a little,' a Korrigan said looking down towards his waist. 'Oh! I don't have any pants.'

Another Korrigan stopped and looked at his own waist. 'Me neither.'

The chief Korrigan clipped both their ears. 'He's a Falzard. That's what he is. Just look at the spoon.'

Fizbar felt deflated and embarrassed. He knew he was a wizard; he knew he was worthy of respect and he didn't need to prove it. As he thrust his arms down in a surly manner, a force of wind left his wand thrusting him backwards until he hit a wall. The cage behind the hunchback rattled, shaking violently, but this time the Korrigans weren't the ones doing it. They darted around inside like angry bees. They began to whimper, shriek and cry in succession before finally breaking out into loud howls of fright. The metal chain broke and whipped around in the air like an angry snake. The hunchback walked over to it without taking his eyes off it. The cage hovered a little higher until the hunchback was just under it. The Korrigans cried as the cage fell, hitting the hunchback hard on the hump. The cage was propelled one way, the hunchback and his torch went the other. Then the chamber fell silent again and the flicker of the torch settled.

Fizbar hauled himself up and sat L-shaped on the floor. He shook his head and touched it noticing a bump on the back. He searched for his wand and sighed in relief to find it was within arm's length. He picked it up and looked around to see what had occurred. It had all happened so quickly. To his right a moan drifted from the foot of the bench. The hunchback moved slightly. He came around slowly, mumbling unclear and confused words. The wizard looked at the cage to his left and it was empty. The hatch door was wide open, but there were no Korrigans inside. Fizbar felt relieved but wasn't sure what had happened. To be honest, he didn't care either.

'Are you all right?' asked the spoon in a hushed tone.

Fizbar nodded.

'I don't want to sound rude but I believe the spell you might have been looking for was *Evanesco*, the banishing spell. Would have been much easier than an unrehearsed vanishing spell. It would also have been a little less painful.'

'Well if you had taught…'

'Fizbar?' said the spoon in a low resonant tone.

'What?'

'Aren't you forgetting something?'

'What?'

'The hunchback. Surely he's going to eat us now. I'm a spoon! Oh my God! He will use me to eat you—'

'Don't be stupid!' It was the wizard's turn to cut short. 'He's getting up…'

The moan got louder and the hunchback slowly began to lift himself to his feet. Rubbing his neck he attempted to look over his shoulder. He noticed that his hump was back to normal size. A smile grew on his face. Fizbar covered his eyes with his hands and was about to speak, but the hunchback spoke first.

'Thank you!' He walked over to the wizard. 'Thank you, thank you, thank you, thank you.'

Fizbar still felt uneasy. He didn't dare move. The hunchback might eat him seeing he could now move a little faster than before. He wasn't convinced the "thank yous" would keep him safe. 'Are you going to eat me?' he asked earnestly.

The hunchback stared at him. 'Why do you ask?' he said frowning. His accent was clearer now that his temper was back to normal, and his pronunciation Northern, definitely not Sintarian.

'I am extremely thin and wouldn't really satisfy your belly. I'm also not sure what happens when a wizard gets eaten.' His face now long and deadpan; hesitantly he bit his finger. 'But I don't really want to find out either.'

'Why would I eat someone who has just helped me?' He pointed to his hump. 'It's back to normal.' He managed a short guttural laugh. Fizbar didn't find it funny, and his expression was wooden.

'I mean you're still angry enough to flatten me like a sheet of paper because I'm a wizard. You know, after what happened all those years ago.' His bottom was cold from the stone floor so he lifted himself and continued in a timid tone whilst pointing at the cage, 'but I am a powerful wizard I might add!'

The hunchback rubbed his shoulder, then his hump. A sharp pain made his face twitch. It ached. It hurt. He continued rubbing his back, trying to find a comfortable position. Fizbar looked around. The space was empty apart from a large sack at the end of the stone bench. The only noise was sporadic drips of water falling from the ceiling. Fizbar broke the silence.

'May I ask you a question?'

The hunchback nodded.

'Is your brother really…'

'Handsome?' He cut the wizard short. He pronounced the word beautifully with softness and finesse. 'Not like me.'

The hunchback looked unhappy with the comparison. Fizbar swallowed. The hunchback looked transfixed, continuing to caress his hump. He began to sympathise with his burden. 'Yes.' He straightened his back wincing at the discomfort before shuffling round to face Fizbar.

'For a little thing you ask some strange questions.'

'He has that habit. He's been like it ever since I met him,' the spoon blurted out.

Fizbar shook him sternly, the wand made a spluttering sound. 'There, that should wipe that smile off your wooden face.'

The hunchback sniggered. Fizbar and his wand stopped their bickering as they watched the hunchback walk to the cage and pick it up. He stared at it vacantly, tapping the little door, pushing it back and forth as it swung open and closed. 'I miss this.'

'Miss what?' asked Fizbar as he moved stealthily like a cat towards the bench.

'*Stay well away and don't get too close,*' muttered his wand. Fizbar banged his right pocket, suggesting that the wand be quiet.

'Miss the companionship we once had with wizards and their talking wands.' He glanced back at Fizbar. 'The good ones I mean.'

The hunchback then dropped the cage. It made a loud, tinny clang, just like a suit of armour hitting the floor. It made Fizbar jump and he leapt up from the bench before turning, and sitting back down. The hunchback gave the wizard a disfavouring look.

'By the way, my name is Fizbar,' he said gesturing with an open hand. The hunchback ignored him and looked back at the cage; then he spoke with a snivel. 'Meedril.'

Fizbar assumed that was his name. 'What are you looking for, Meedril?'

'Chocolate… Those blighters ate every last crumb.'

'Chocolate?'

The hunchback didn't reply. Instead he trundled over to the sack that was next to the bench. Fizbar shuffled to the end of the bench, still unsure and a little anxious.

'How did you manage to find those awful little creatures?' Fizbar thought quickly to change from quizzing the hunchback. 'I've been here before, you know?'

'When?'

'I can't for the life of me remember… But I've never seen any Korrigans. I'd much prefer to see fairies.' Fizbar scratched his head, and then patted the bump on his head which was still there. Then he felt dizzy. A tingle crept up his wand arm and a vision danced in his mind, swaying trees, fierce winds and a gathering of hunchbacks holding torches in the heavy and slanting rain. His head pounded but he managed to force his eyes open and as he released the grasp on his wand, the vision left as quickly as it had come.

'Are you all right?' asked the hunchback.

'It's nothing. I just hit my head and this bump is killing me.' He picked up his spoon.

'Here.' The hunchback wiped his mouth with a rag and handed it to Fizbar. 'Place it on your bump. It'll help.'

Fizbar's face exuded disgust and he shuddered when the goo touched his skin. The funny thing was the instant soothing effect and Fizbar's astonishment turned to relief.

'You've got to get them really angry to turn into Korrigan's. It's a horrible form. You can't reason with 'em.'

'I'm surprised you got them into that cage in the first place.' He pointed at the broken birdcage.

The hunchback smiled at it. 'It wasn't difficult.' He wiped his nose and green sticky saliva spread along his sleeve from his elbow to his wrist. He snorted and then swallowed.

Fizbar heard the lump travel down his throat, and upturned his nose whilst looking away.

'Ma brother met someone in the forest,' the hunchback continued. 'He said that he worked for ma master. Told him Korrigans loved chocolate. I stuck some in that cage. Simple as that. Like rats they went for it.'

'I think chocolate is truly irresistible to any living creature,' said Fizbar with a smile.

The hunchback's stern face didn't change, 'I think he thought ma brother was me,' he said. Then his expression turned to sadness.

'Who?' asked Fizbar with interest.

'The person in the forest. I always told ma master that I wished he could help me get rid of this hump. He never helped. He said I'm a hunchback and should live with it.' He pointed to it with a darting finger, as if in disgust. 'It was the only thing I ever wanted. He told ma brother he wanted to reunite hunchbacks. Ma master... Ma master... He wants... He wants...' He broke into confusing muttering.

'You met your master in the forest?' Fizbar inquired trying not to interrupt the flow of what seemed like a confession. He hoped his persistence wouldn't upset the large figure in front of him.

'No, not ma master, a servant of his.' He wet his lips, wiping more saliva from his lower lip. He also wiped his nose with the other arm. 'That was better days then, before the revolt. Before hunchbacks fought against their masters.' He huffed firmly, his tone nervous. He sneezed. A large shot of snot flew across the room. Fizbar now felt sick. 'Not me. I'd never do that. Never fight against ma master.'

'Who *was* your master? Why do you mention the revolt?'

The hunchback shook his head wiping away the memories and started to become irritable at Fizbar's pressing line of questioning.

'And what's it to you, ay? Why do ya want to know?

Do ya want to know his name? Huh! Wizards are all the same at heart… But ma master, he's different, Meedril knows that. In our native tongue the hunchbacks call him, Rordorack.'

Fizbar spoke out of the corner of his mouth down at his wand, carefully so the hunchback wouldn't hear. '*Thought you said they weren't stupid. He's bonkers.*'

'Rordorack? Who is he?' the wizard humoured him.

The hunchback's face changed; it was weathered and beastly. A remaining lock of black clumped hair fell down his right cheek. 'Enough! Meedril says enough! No more questions. Ask the Lex Talionis! That's who was in the forest. Now off with you. You and ya spoon! Ma belly's rumbling and I might just change ma mind!'

'*I think we should leave,*' whispered his wand; a tremor in its tone. Fizbar didn't want to. He wanted to persist with his line of inquiry, especially since the hunchback had mentioned the Lex Talionis. He was hungry for more information, but on reflection didn't favour playing the role of a piece of chocolate himself.

'*What are you doing?*' said his spoon quietly as Fizbar pointed him upwards.

'*Going to cast a spell to get us out of here. What you suggested at the very beginning.*'

The spoon spoke. '*I think it may be safer for us to walk. I think you do need the exercise after all.*'

8

An Untimely Letter

Fizbar tossed and turned in bed, unable to sleep. For a few minutes he lay in bed thinking about Rordorack and the Lex Talionis. He had not studied languages at school and Ranarrack, the language of the hunchbacks, was virtually unknown to him. He thought back wishing he had chosen this stream of the course. But the rest of his contemplation focused on the Lex Talionis. He knew that Zalbar was the head of the group that was usually responsible for all the crime and wrongdoings in Sintar as well as further across the land. Fizbar felt dispirited that the majority of members of this group were Falzards. It's because of the Lex that people frown and narrow their eyes at me when I bring out the spoon, he thought.

His eyes now welcomed the light and with open arms he yawned, stretched and then swung himself over the side of the bed before finally lifting himself up and into his slippers. He walked sleepily towards the window and banged his head on a low beam that hung half a metre below the ceiling. Instead of shouting with a large OUCH! he grunted, followed by another sleepy yawn, as his night hat had padded him from the blow. His pyjamas were mostly white, but patterns of large blue stars were scattered like seeds. He looked out at the window and noticed the sun rising quickly. A little too quickly, or was it the fact that today he was slower than normal in getting out of bed. He unlocked the double-hung window and lifted it upwards catching the tip of his hat.

Fizbar glanced down at the town, admiring the movements of the Sintarians. Like ants in a colony, everybody had a job, had a duty; had things to do. He noticed a young boy dressed in brown with a leather satchel over his shoulder. He ran from the foot of his door not looking back as he sped off towards the tavern across the street before vanishing round the corner. Fizbar didn't think too hard about it, it wasn't out of the ordinary; couriers and post-boys were frequently at his door delivering requests for odd jobs that only a wizard could do.

He took a deep breath of the clean, fresh air whilst rubbing his stomach and moving his lips at the slight waft of fried bacon. He was hungry, so he closed the window without noticing that his hat had caught on the latch and stayed there. Today he felt different. He felt content and after yesterday's performance with the hunchback, he oozed confidence. His night had been untroubled and without any peculiar dreams or flashbacks. A new day brought a new mood; he was happy and stress free. Unanswered questions still lingered about the hunchback, but he was already thinking about new jobs, wondering what the Council would allocate him next. His feeling of elation was fuelled by that fact that more jobs meant a step closer to becoming a second level wizard. It would come soon enough, but the end of his first year as a wizard was still a long way away and Falzards had a more difficult job in advancing than others. In fact no Falzard had ever moved up the career ladder past second level. Then his smile dropped and was replaced by a musing countenance.

Walking to the landing he failed to notice a lip in the carpet and tripped, which launched him down the stairs. He tumbled and landed face down in front of the doormat. He let out a small groan and his eyes slowly rolled back to normal. There in front of his nose was a neatly hand-folded paper and on the top of it was a large, red, wax seal. He jumped up, picked it up and inspected it. It was the seal of the Overlord. He examined it closer, thinking it might be a prank; wondering why Therolius Delrunt would send him a letter, or anything for that matter. It was genuine but the scent of fried bacon was stronger than any Overlord-related urgency, and he decided to leave it until after breakfast. He popped it into his pocket and made for the kitchen, but as he walked the urge to open it became overpowering. He grabbed a letter opener from the hall table and carefully prized open the elegant letter. The handwriting was also elegant. The specific letters were beautifully rounded with regular spacing and the text read:

Dear Fizbar,

You may be aware that Sintar is not the place it once used to be. Especially with horrid attacks that torment the very heart of our wizarding society.

I have an urgent matter I wish to discuss with you. I would be most grateful if you would meet me at my office at lunchtime today.

With every best assurance,

Therolius Delrunt.

Overlord.

P.S. Don't tell anyone about our meeting.

P.S.S. Now throw the letter in front of you, quickly!

Fizbar held the letter with his index finger and thumb and without hesitation threw it into the air. The letter popped and vanished, leaving only a small cloud of dust which fell languidly to the floor, and then fizzled away.

'Hmm.' Fizbar pondered. 'Why would the Overlord want to see me?' he paused. 'I hope I haven't done anything wrong.'

'Not sure. You didn't cheat on your exams did you?' asked the spoon.

'Morning to you too, and certainly not!' replied Fizbar wholeheartedly. He couldn't believe his wand would even suggest such a thing.

'It must be important if he's enchanted a letter. Vanishing letters are only used if it's meant for one set of eyes. Well, apart from the writer's.'

'It's true,' he smiled, thinking of the implications of that. 'Maybe I'm being recruited into a secret crime fighting unit of wizards.'

'I doubt that. Wizards are the crime fighting unit.'

'That's true,' said Fizbar half-annoyed and half-relieved. 'What about a position at the school as a teacher?'

'You're not weird enough for that,' said the wand. 'On second thoughts…'

'Er… Why?' said Fizbar, noticing his own voice sounding strange.

'You're still very young, Master,' the spoon pointed out quickly to save his own skin.

'Fine,' said Fizbar half-amused and half irritated. 'But what else could it be?'

'I don't know, but there's only one way to find out'

'What's that?'

'We'd better get a move on.'

'Why?' Fizbar looked at the clock on his wall. It was made out of wood and designed in the shape of three coloured books yellow, red and blue. Its hands were deliberately buckled, but pointed to the right time –11a.m. 'You're right. We'd better get going.' He reached for the handle of the front door and turned it. His wand coughed continuously, hinting to the wizard.

'What?' said Fizbar.

'I know I can't see, but I do believe you are still in your moon pyjamas.'

Fizbar looked down. 'Oh! Yes, you're right.' He darted back up the stairs.

'Hurry up!' the spoon shouted. 'You can't be late for the Overlord.'

9

A Gift from Therolius Delrunt

The school looked the same. It had only been three months since Fizbar had left. What had changed was Fizbar himself. He was no longer a student and saw the school and its surroundings with different eyes. On entering the building he felt the student buzz, with affection, but also with sadness at the thought of leaving it all behind. He walked along the winding corridor passing his old classrooms and for a moment peered into one of them. It was empty and dark. It would only be an hour until the school was back in full swing, but it didn't look that way. He put his mouth to the glass door and blew. It would have been funny amongst other students, although there was nobody there to laugh at it. He chuckled to himself and continued on. The corridor was long. It started at the entrance and wound all the way to the top, just like a curling snake. No stairs in this school; no need for them. It was a wizard's school. A strange wind prevented you from falling back down. Fizbar loved this about the school and was glad to be back, just for that particular experience he dearly missed.

He approached the last bend and panted a little at the climb; his wand was silent. He recalled the last time he had been sent to the Overlord's office and he knew the steepness of the climb only too well; so did his legs. It deterred many students from misbehaving. The corridor was silent except for the odd sound of a typewriter clicking, the echo almost lasting long enough to overlap with the next click. It was Mrs Sonia Dewfont, the secretary. She was a small, old lady, very thin and always dressed in a green or red tartan suit with matching lipstick. Today it was green. A red hat with a green bobble in the middle sat on her head like a bake-well tart. Her white hair covered each ear like large earmuffs. She had finished typing and had arranged a pile of papers on her desk neatly. She grabbed her handbag and noticed Fizbar approaching.

'Mr Trundle. How nice it is to see you again,' she said smiling.

'Nice to see you again Mrs Dewfont,' he replied courteously.

'I was just about to pop out for a spot of lunch. Is there anything I can do for you?'

Fizbar assumed she knew nothing of the letter.

'I've come to see the Overlord.'

'Oh!' she replied. 'I don't think…' she opened her diary and ran her finger down the page before turning over and repeating the action.

'I'll take it from here, Mrs Dewfont.'

Therolius stood by the half-open door to his office. It startled Sonia a little. Even Fizbar hadn't seen him appear. She paused briefly. 'In that case, Overlord I'll be off home for a bite to eat. Got to get Mr Dewfont's lunch ready.'

Therolius smiled. 'Thank you, and please wish him well from me.'

Mrs Dewfont hovered inquisitively for a couple of seconds, flicking her eyes from the Overlord to Fizbar. She wondered about the secret rendezvous. Therolius could always trust Mrs Dewfont, and whatever she witnessed usually went no further. That's why he had chosen her as his secretary. She placed the diary in the bottom drawer of her desk and slowly sauntered off. She didn't even turn around for a sneak peak.

'Please, Fizbar,' said the Overlord welcoming him into his office.

As the Overlord closed the door quietly behind him, Fizbar sat down on a chair opposite the large desk. Therolius peered through his spy-hole in the door for extra assurance. It was a special spy-hole that could see all the way down the spiral corridor. When he saw Mrs Dewfont leave the front door, he walked over and sat behind his desk. He dipped into his left cloak pocket and pulled out his wand. He placed it on the table to one side and Fizbar watched it, not taking his eyes off it for a second. He had always liked the Overlord's wand and smiled warmly. But that was cut short with a shameful thought of his own wand and Therolius picked up on it.

'A wand is a wand no matter the appearance. It's the guide in him which counts.'

Fizbar didn't reply. He had no riposte, and Therolius seized the moment to draw a small brown leather journal from his other pocket, and then placed it on the table in front of him; and with care. It was worn and the pages were thick and uneven. Odd pages poked from the fore edge. Fizbar turned his head to focus on the journal, noticing four raised bands on the spine and gilt lettering on the front board. He narrowed his brow and leant forward a little, but couldn't make it out. He looked back to the wand before the Overlord spoke, drawn again by its majestic shape, presence and stature as the supreme wand. 'You may be wandering why I have asked you here.'

Fizbar was quiet, his mouth dry. Finally his lips unzipped. 'Well, yes.'

'Me too.' A muffled voice came from his pocket.

Therolius bent around the corner of his desk. 'Thurrock, what a pleasure.'

'The pleasure's all mine, Overlord.'

It was Fizbar's turn to dip into his pocket and he reluctantly placed his spoon on the table.

'Good to see you. I trust you're keeping Fizbar out of harm's way.'

'Without question, Overlord. It's good to hear your voice of reason again.'

Therolius chuckled. 'I've always liked your guide, Fizbar. Right from your days as a tenderfoot.'

'Thank you.' He wasn't impressed with his wand's frankness. 'You seem as though you're old friends,' said Fizbar.

The Overlord chose not to answer.

'Why did you want to see me, Sir?' Fizbar's eyes turned back to the wand, then a quick few seconds on the book.

'As I said in my letter, these are testing times. Sintar is in a state of uncertainty and we all know the Lex Talionis are getting stronger by the day.'

'Yes, it's because of them we Falzard's have a bad name.'

'I wish people would stop using that reference, even collectively. There is no such thing in my book.'

'Not everyone thinks like an Overlord—'

'As I was saying,' said Therolius cutting Fizbar short, 'there were times when magic was pure and respected. Sintarians, regardless of culture, creed or occupation lived in harmony and the city prospered. The Grimoire was put together long ago to equip future generations of wizards with the knowledge needed to enrich this harmony. Little consideration was given to, or perhaps I should say, they underestimated the power of lust, greed, arrogance and pride.'

'Greed?' said Fizbar. 'The powers of evil intent.'

'I know what greed is, Fizbar. There have been wizards that desired The Grimoire from the day it was compiled by the great order of the past. It was recognised for its unique power.' He exhaled noisily. 'Even the wizards that contributed to making The Grimoire needed to show firm resistance. They too feared their own desire for such a powerful book.'

Fizbar's eyes moved to the room that housed The Grimoire. He scanned it hoping to see the famous green glow. 'You mean, Gelorg?' said Fizbar still fixed on the door. 'Wasn't he a good wizard?' He looked at the Overlord, focusing on his nose.

'That's the... How shall I put it, *public* version of the story. When I was ordained as Overlord a small minority of wizards were displeased. Within this minority some of them had thought they would get the position. When none of them did, they contemplated stealing The Grimoire.'

'But they didn't.'

'No, but the point here is that they thought about it. And they could have taken it. Gelorg was not part of the minority. He had his own agenda, but different from the others. He wanted me to know that he could take The Grimoire whenever he wanted.'

'But he didn't?' said Fizbar only half-sure of his answer.

'No. But he revealed insecurities that threatened the book's safety. So, as Overlord I put a spell on it. A spell that only the Overlord or a pure-blood could break.'

'There is no such thing as a pure-blood,' Fizbar responded forcefully.

'Yes there is, Fizbar. A pure-blood has to be proven and sanctioned by the book. It's not down to your blood type, well, not entirely. Anyway the point I'm trying to make is about the power of The Grimoire.'

'Your spell. That's why Zalbar couldn't take it?'

Therolius's face dropped. He was expressionless. 'My spell was aimed at his touch, and that is all. My spell had a holding power. Only I could release whoever had touched it. I had to do what was necessary.' His eyes wondered over to the door.

'I'm not following this conversation. I'm a little confused.'

'The Grimoire is sacred. It's the most powerful object in our kingdom.'

'In the right hands,' said Fizbar, happy with his answer.

'Even in the wrong hands.'

'But you put that spell on it.'

'Yes, but even you know spells can be broken.'

Fizbar scratched his chin. 'As well as Zalbar there is also someone called "Rordorack". Do you know who he is?'

Therolius's face changed. This time his expression was wide and overwrought. 'I believe "Rordorack" is Zalbar. I've heard it's what the hunchbacks call him.'

'So the hunchback was talking about Zalbar?'

'Hunchback?' Therolius crumpled his forehead. 'What hunchback?'

'Long story, but why is he called that?'

'What hunchback?' Therolius banged his hand on the table; he was annoyed and rattled.

'The Council gave me a job to help a hunchback deal with some Korrigan's. That's all. After I helped him he told me his master was Rordorack.'

'This isn't good, Fizbar. Nobody must know of this. Who else knows apart from the Council?'

'The people present on the benches I suppose, including Gimera.'

'I'll have to deal with that through other channels. You shouldn't have got that job. These jobs are only given to wizards of the fifth order, the Archmage; or myself.'

'Then why was I given the job?' Fizbar was perplexed but also pleased that he had managed the job of a higher grade.

'I don't know. But I *will* find out.'

'So Rordorack is Zalbar? What does that mean?'

'I believe it's an uprising against me, so Zalbar can mount a resistance that will enable him to finally get his hands on The Grimoire. I cast a spell on him long ago and it's something neither of us can forgive or forget. I feel in some way responsible for turning him into the person he has become. I am worried he is planning something immeasurably evil.'

'What makes you think that?'

'Yesterday I was cornered by a member of the Lex Talionis. He was after something very valuable to his master. I knew what he was after, but managed to resist it being taken.' He tapped the journal. Fizbar felt flushed and he opened his tunic at the neck to let in some cool air. 'This is all very thrilling, but what does this have to do with me?'

'Here.' Therolius poured a glass of water for him. 'You look as though you could do with it.' Then he brought out a bottle of whiskey from a drawer and poured one for himself. 'The fact is young wizard, that it affects all of us. Wizard and non-wizard alike. As the capital, Sintar has become the base of the Lex Talionis. Worryingly, I have heard of followers as far as Fintar. My contacts there say there is an increasing amount of crime and skirmishes between wizards and non-wizards. The psychics are confused; they can't make any sense of the matter.'

'That's a first.' Fizbar grunted.

'It is a first; you're right. It's also serious and terribly troubling. If they are confused then how are we to know what's to come? If their minds are clouded it can only mean that something or someone is clouding them.'

'Are you suggesting Zalbar is the reason for all of this?'

'I know he is. With new recruits to the Lex Talionis it is only a matter of time before another rebellion starts.'

Fizbar looked away, and then scratched an itchy eyebrow. 'Another rebellion, like the hunchbacks of long ago?'

Therolius looked Fizbar in the eye. 'It wasn't that long ago, but this one will be even worse.'

'I'm not sure what this story has to do with me?'

Therolius straightened his back and lifted the little brown book. With a whisper he said, 'This is Zalbar's journal.'

Fizbar felt winded. His mouth dried. He pointed. 'That book is…'

'Yes. It is.'

'How did you get it?' said Fizbar anxiously as he looked around for stray eyes; even ears.

'I've always had it. Ever since Zalbar…' Like Fizbar he too looked for words in thin air and changed his tone, '… Left school.'

'But he didn't leave school. We all know the stories.'

'Unfortunately, that's one malicious rumour which is undeniably true. But nobody knows I have his journal in my possession. I am sure Zalbar has his suspicions, ever since the book opened unavoidably after our,' his head danced, 'duel… But he can't pinpoint its exact location.'

'Then neither can his cronies. But I still don't understand why you're telling me this?'

'I have a job for you, Fizbar. I need you to take this journal and hide it. Keep it safe.'

Fizbar lifted himself off the chair quickly, as if he had sat on a hot heater or had been stung by a hornet. 'I'm not doing that! He'll find me; he'll… He'll…'

'Calm down. He won't know you'll have it. All you have to do is keep it safe, and keep it shut! Please Fizbar. He won't suspect you ever having it if you follow these simple instructions.'

'What about the Archmage? Can't he help you?'

'I can't trust anybody, Fizbar.'

Fizbar crossed his arms and turned to face the Overlord. 'And you trust me all of a sudden?'

'There is more to you Fizbar Trundle than plain old trust. You're scared, and that's perfectly acceptable. In this case it's a quality I value.'

'It's because nobody would suspect a Falzard isn't it?' said Fizbar at once before slumping back in his chair. He didn't want to take the journal. He could get up and just walk out of the office as if this meeting had never happened. 'What's to stop me from refusing?' he asked, his leg moving up and down as if he'd had twelve coffees. He hoped he had the upper hand.

'Nothing. You can walk out of here any time.' Therolius tilted his head. 'However, I implore you to please at least consider. I have my reasons for choosing you.'

'And they are?'

Therolius didn't answer as he stared at Fizbar.

'What do I have to do? What do I get in return?' Fizbar

asked pointing his finger at his own chest. He expected at the very least an opportunity to boost his chances of advancing in the wizarding ranks. Therolius knew this, smiled and played on it. He knew Fizbar better than the young wizard thought.

'I'm sure we can come to some kind of agreement. A proposal perhaps?'

'I'm listening.'

'I would have thought helping the Overlord would be reward enough, but if you manage to keep this book from Zalbar, you may be able to climb the wizarding ladder quicker than anyone has ever done before.'

'No Falzard has climbed even to the second level.'

'So you will be the first. What better way to restore the good name and prestige. I sincerely hope you stop using that reference. It's very ugly and insulting.'

'I'd take the book if I were you,' said the spoon.

Fizbar stared at the spoon with a blank expression, deep in thought. There was something else about the wand, a certain sparkle, but Fizbar couldn't quite work out what it meant, so he didn't reply.

As Therolius took a sip of whiskey, he slowly pushed the book forwards across the table, and Fizbar reluctantly picked it up. 'You must never open it. Just keep it safe and you'll be fine.'

'Why not?'

'It's safer that way.'

'If I accept, when do you want it back?'

'Never,' said Therolius in a calm and low voice.

Fizbar ran his fingers over the journal. The lettering written in felt-pen read: *The Binding Journal*. He looked at Therolius and noticed a stressed look. He was pale and tired. Fizbar felt a deep-seated urge to help him. How difficult could it be to hide a journal? 'What does this mean? Binding Journal?'

'I don't know.'

Fizbar wasn't sure he was telling the truth, but as he was the Overlord Fizbar could hardly accuse him of not being truthful. 'All right; on one condition.'

'And what is that?'

'You answer a question.'

'Which is?'

There was a short pause.

'Why doesn't your wand speak to you?'

There was a longer pause as the Overlord stared at his wand. He ran his finger over the wood, stroking it, feeling the smooth surface. 'It's a long story my dear boy.'

'A concise version then.'

Therolius's facial expression revealed the furrows on both sides of his mouth. He gently reached for his wand. Fizbar sensed a tight feeling of distress. With watery eyes the Overlord finally spoke. 'Ever since I caused pain to a child. A wizarding child, my wand has become silent. She has never spoken to me since that day, here in this very same office.'

'The day you... And Zalbar?'

The Overlord nodded as if in shame overlaid by grief. Tears swelled in his eyes. Fizbar thought that perhaps he shouldn't have asked a question that now appeared insensitive. It was obviously a painful memory, something the Overlord clearly didn't want to remember.

'Well then, I'd better get this off to a safe place,' he waved the journal in the air.

Therolius looked up, his watery eyes glistening in the light. 'Thank you, Fizbar. And I also have this for you.' He handed over an ornate iron key the size of a hairpin.

'What's it for?' Fizbar asked in bewilderment.

'You'll know when the time is right.'

Without thinking he took the key from the Overlord and popped it into his pocket along with his wand.

'Here we go again. Into the pocket,' said the spoon.

'I have just one more question to ask.' Fizbar spoke confidently, and with a hint of good will.

'Something else you want me to confess to?'

Therolius got up and walked over to the window. He moved a curtain to one side as he peered down over the bustling town below.

'Oh no, just to see if you're going to Helena Elantari's opening of the newly refurbished *The Magic Garden* I hear she has some new swamp plants and other goodies. I know you have a fondness for natural history and all that.'

'Oh yes... Helena... Yes, I'll be there. In fact I've been asked to open it.' Therolius didn't move his head from the view.

'Great! I guess I'll see you there then,' he said, not expecting a reply. He popped the book into his pocket almost carelessly.

Therolius felt for a moment that giving such an important book to Fizbar was a bad idea. He restrained himself, as it had to be done. 'Please keep it safe, Fizbar.' Therolius beamed back at him.

Fizbar walked to the door and turned the handle half way before stopping. 'You know something?'

'And what is that?'

'It wasn't your fault.'

A hollow smile crept onto the Overlord's face as Fizbar closed the door behind him. Then he muttered to himself. '*If only you knew the rest my dear boy.*'

Fizbar took the journal out of his pocket and stared at it for a few seconds, wondering about its importance. Why had the Overlord trusted him with the book? He ran his fingers lightly over the lettering *The Binding Journal* before placing it back in his pocket and heading off around the corner of the school and out of sight. Across the road a figure that had been keeping a close eye on Fizbar approached the kerb. He removed his hood, which revealed the face of the Archmage; it was Gimera. He smiled and looked up at the Overlord's window before leaving in the opposite direction to the one in which Fizbar had gone. Just as the Archmage blended into the crowd another figure appeared from a shadowed spot. It was Gildor, Fizbar's old teacher. He looked nervous as always and he had seen both Gimera and Fizbar. He twitched and pulled his waistcoat straight before walking across the road, nearly getting knocked over by a horse and cart. He ran quickly to the front of the school, took off his spectacles and entered.

10

Failure and Failures

A cloaked figure in forest green paced up and down towards the end of a throne room, one hand behind his back and the other gripping his crooked staff. A thick brown belt with a silver buckle was fastened tightly around his willowy waist. He finally stopped at the end of a raised platform, his stage. He stood in front of a large granite lectern and with one hand caressed it as if appreciating a great book that was obviously missing. Three shrouded men entered the room with their leader out in front. They approached cautiously; their movements showing signs of hesitation. The green-cloaked figure glanced over his shoulder, but a hood covered his identity. Oil lamps in bowls stood tall on stands and suspended from the roof in rings, providing better illumination. Some flares hung from the iron rings in the walls that were common in castles. He focused on the men entering his warmly lit sanctuary. His posture astute and at the same time disdainful and threatening.

'Lord Zalbar, we have finally located the fourth journal.

It is closer than we first thought. Very close in fact,' said the leader as they continued walking along a green carpet, and past wooden benches similar to that of a church. Their walk was cut short when they reached the foot of the platform. They hoped that the news would create a more relaxed atmosphere.

Zalbar turned immediately, head stooped; his identity still concealed. He raised a hand urging them to stop and the leader swallowed hard, his anxiety reaching a new level. Zalbar lifted his head. A smoky, darkness lurked where his face should have been. The swirls appeared like spirits trapped in time, levitating, hovering, lost and trying to find a way out. The two men that flanked the leader knelt, whilst the leader remained on his feet. He was a faun. His goat-like appearance merged with a human physique, which looked unnatural as well as impressive.

In a dark and crispy tone Zalbar spoke. 'Did you say, first thought? I must point out that you are not here to think. You should be using every effort in procuring that journal!'

'My Lord, we have just learned of this news ourselves from the farrier we brought in for questioning. He *was* telling the truth after all, he didn't know of the journal's location. It was his wife who finally came forward and told us. Apparently she works for the owner of the journal.'

'Medra Fanbar?' asked Zalbar in a light and inquisitive voice.

'Yes Lord?' he replied, his tone nervous and fearful.

'I want that journal!' He raised his voice and the sound echoed in the great hall. Then he raised his arm and a curly, dark tanned wand pointed straight at the faun's head.

'But Lord…'

'*CINEFACTUS!*' shouted Zalbar and a fiery red beam shot from the tip of his wand. The faun's eyes bulged to the size of golf balls, before he burst into red ash. There were a tense few seconds as the ash slowly drifted and hit the carpet. As it did, the ash vanished. Zalbar focused on the remaining men. Zalbar composed himself. 'If I don't have that journal soon I will have no alternative but to relieve you both of your positions. Now, are you incapable of bringing it to me?' He spoke quickly, waiting for a favourable response. He tucked his wand into the sleeve of his cloak. The men looked at each other, a little relieved but still sweating with fear. 'Maybe I should award your incompetencies with early retirement just like your faun friend, hmm? You're lucky, this is my forgiving mood,' said Zalbar with cruel disregard. The atmosphere in the room now reeked of terror. One man looked at the floor, the other followed his lead.

'If I may, Lord Zalbar,' asked one man cautiously. The other glanced at him, afraid of the possible consequences of this action. The sweat trickled down his black and bushy brow. He wiped his forehead and as he did this he felt cold and uncomfortable as his shirt touched his soaked back.

'You may, Denrick. But I urge you to think before you speak.'

'... You *will* have the journal my Lord; I guarantee it, before the night is over.' The sweat ran faster down his forehead. He wiped it then looked at his wet fingers. He could feel the warmth surge from within but he was cold and his shirt was now soaking, but he managed to control his breathing and retain a little composure.

'Good! That's better. Let me just remind you that if you fail, I will have more than your heads, *I guarantee that.* Use the goats if you must!' Zalbar flicked his wand at Denrick then at two of the faun guards that stood on either side of the large wooden doors at the end of the hall. The men lifted themselves quickly off the floor, turned and shuffled out of the room before Zalbar could change his mind. Two fauns opened the door and Denrick gestured for them to follow him. They departed, leaving the subtle noise of hooves on the carpet.

Zalbar sighed heavily and out of the darkness appeared a hunched figure with long arms. Zalbar's temper remained unabated as his boney and long fingered hand began to glow. His cupped hand exuded a faint crimson lustre, and he shook his head in self-pity.

'I hate fauns!' stressed the figure as it stepped out of the shadows into full view. It was a hunchback.

Zalbar ignored his statement. 'We need all six journals

before we can perform the ritual, Meedril. I have one tricky obstacle standing in my way.'

'Who?'

'Therolius Delrunt. The runt of all wizards.'

Meedril let out a feeble and unconvincing snigger. His laughter was muffled, but still out of place. Zalbar walked past a tall chair; then to the lectern, which boasted a gold canopy. Once again he stood in front of it. To one side was a lit candle that was drawing to a faint and feeble flicker. Zalbar extinguished it with a skeletal hand that showed no signs of pain from the naked flame. 'Never underestimate your enemy Meedril. The laws of success are just as cold-hearted as those for failure. It's the failure that you learn more from. Not success,' said Zalbar before turning to face the hunchback.

Meedril flinched. Zalbar's face always startled him. 'Sire, you have three journals and the fourth is within your grasp. The time is nearing and revenge is at hand.' He continued whilst shoving a large finger into his nose.

'I wish you wouldn't do that. It's disgusting and undignified,' said Zalbar, shaking his head with displeasure.

'I'm a hunchback, Sire, there is nothing graceful about us.' Meedril pulled the finger out of his nose and wiped the contents of the excavation on his knee-high trousers.

Zalbar sighed in disgust. The air suddenly became dense and Zalbar looked to the foot of his platform. A smoky figure manifested in front of him. 'Ah! The Badger returns. Please do not disappoint me Viktor. I'm in no mood for disappointments.'

The tattered pirate adjusted his eye patch and his posture, realigning his spine. His head was bent forwards but his eyes focused firmly on Zalbar.

'My lord,' he cleared his throat, 'I confronted Therolius but...'

'Not another one! Do I have to do *everything* myself?'

'No,' Viktor replied in haste.

'That was a rhetorical question.' He walked down the steps slowly, closer to Viktor, ready to hear his full confession. Viktor started to fidget; twitching his fingers and his neck. Zalbar scared him. Zalbar scared everyone and Viktor didn't want to disappoint him. Zalbar moved closer until his smoky void of a face was inches from Viktor's ear. He whispered clearly and Viktor's eyes flew to the left. 'Do... You... Have it?' Zalbar sounded impatient.

Viktor's lips trembled; he felt the urge to run away. He thought of an answer, but there was no other except for the truth. 'No.'

Zalbar roared as he went for his wand. Viktor puffed into smoke, but reappeared further down the corridor, flickering.

'But I know he has it. I will get it. I promise!' said Viktor fearing Zalbar's moves and gestures. He kept a close eye on his wand.

'So many promises yet they are never fulfilled. Sometimes I wonder why the Lex Talionis exists if they CAN'T DO THEIR WORK PROPERLY!' Zalbar shouted again. The windows in the hall were equipped with wooden shutters secured by iron bars and they rattled at Zalbar's outrage.

Viktor shied away like a frightened mouse. He pushed his white lock of hair back from his face. 'Sire, it's Therolius. He's very powerful and…'

'Are we making excuses now Viktor?' said Zalbar with a lordly tone.

'No,' he replied, waiting attentively for Zalbar's response.

'What pains me Viktor, is that if I got rid of all you buffoons, I'd have nobody left to aid me.'

'We do want to help—'

'I said aid, not help,' Zalbar cut in, flicking his wand at him.

Viktor noticed something strange about Zalbar's wand. He took a couple of deep breaths, building his defence, choosing his words carefully. 'The word on the street, Lord Zalbar, is that the Magic Garden is opening its doors after an extensive renovation. Therolius is opening it personally. I can—'

'You won't do anything.' He cut Viktor short. 'Let them have their ceremony, it'll be short lived anyway.'

'And Therolius?' He dared not look at Zalbar's void of a face.

'I'll deal with Therolius personally, especially as all of my servants are hopeless nitwits.' Zalbar turned and stared at Viktor who felt his burning gaze. He lifted his wand and flicked it a few times at Viktor who shied away as if a bright light had blinded him. 'I will be meeting him very soon indeed. I have a plan.'

Viktor didn't risk a comment or say anything in response. He remained silent. Zalbar lowered his hand. Viktor noticed his wand was strapped to his forearm. He wasn't holding it; which was unusual. Viktor was curious as well as perturbed.

'Lord, do you know who has the fourth journal?' asked Viktor still wondering about Zalbar's wand.

'Yes.' He replied in a snake-like whisper.

'And the fifth journal?'

'Yes I do.'

'The sixth journal?' He asked again almost boldly.

Zalbar nodded.

'Then…'

'What about my journal?'

'Yes Lord Zalbar, the seventh journal.' Viktor replied dramatically. 'Do you know where it is?'

'That one still eludes me. All I need is for it to be revealed to me. I'm sure Therolius knows what will happen if it is opened.' He looked again at his boney hand, the glow lucid and calm.

'My hand tells me the time is close. Very close indeed.' His tone almost playful.

'Lord, what about the herbalist and the re-opening of her shop?'

'Why do you persist with that wretched shop? Are you into herbs now?'

'No, it's just that, I mean, maybe, and I mean maybe…'

'Will you stop your mumblings and get to the point!'

Viktor's head tilted. 'Maybe all the journals will be there. Everything in one place,' he suggested in a panicky voice. 'Every notable Sintarian must have been invited.' he added.

'But you forget one thing,' he cut short The Badger yet again, 'It will raise too much suspicion and Therolius is not stupid. Old maybe, but only a fool would underestimate him. And a shop full of high-ranking wizards may prove a trifle too much at this present time. No. We have to be calm and collected. I need to plan this carefully.' His hand made for his face, where his chin would have been as he remembered vividly what had happened to him all those years ago at school, when he was a boy, 'I need you to accompany Denrick and Dinfar.'

'The Hex brothers?' he asked, his voice carrying a hint of loathing.

'Yes. You'll assist them by paying Gildor a visit. I need you to extract some information from him. He's Sintar's historian and he knows more than people give him credit for. Especially concerning The Grimoire. Blah!' Zalbar spat. 'He was a horrid and boring little teacher, but he's well known for keeping things to himself. We just need to extract the right bit of information.'

Viktor nodded; then bowed. He was thankful he had escaped Zalbar's wrath and short temper, this time. Although he wasn't sure what information he was to extract, he turned and took no time in vanishing into thin air leaving only strands of smoke heavy on the air. Zalbar thought to himself. The journals were closer than ever before and all were in Sintar. Surely nobody could stop him? It was only a matter of time. He felt a warm smile creep over his invisible face, and failure was far from his mind.

Fizbar drank the last drops from his cup and left the cafeteria thinking about the journal. It sat in his pocket and he felt tempted to bring it out.

'I don't like it here,' said his wand. 'I have a horrible feeling.'

Fizbar dipped into his pocket, pulled out his wand and placed it neatly in the other pocket. 'There! Feel better?'

'That's not what I meant.'

'Then what?'

'It just feels... Evil!'

'It belongs to Zalbar so it's not going to be good is it?'

said Fizbar coldly.

'I know, but there is something more to this journal,' replied his wand, still with an uncomfortable tone.

'Look!' Fizbar pulled the journal from his pocket in frustration and opened it, 'There's nothing wrong—' Suddenly a large screech filled the air and the wind became violent. The journal fell to the floor and the pages flicked from one side to the other, page after page. Fizbar looked for the journal, squinting his eyes against the wind, which prevented him from opening them fully before finally locating it. He leapt onto it and noticed the blank pages before shutting it firmly. The wind departed as quickly as it had come, and a last hiss followed a whisper... *Finally! I know where you are...*

'What the—'

'I told you I had a bad feeling,' the wand cut him short. 'You didn't listen to Therolius did you? You opened it!'

Fizbar realised the carelessness that had resulted from a short burst of frustration caused by a childish tantrum. He hung his head forward in shame and thought for the first time in a long while about his parents. *What would you have done?* he thought, *Nothing! That's what!* He had no one to turn to or ask for guidance. He trusted nobody. He didn't even want to confide in the Overlord. As he wiped away what could have been tears, he thrust the journal back in his pocket. 'I didn't want the bloody journal anyway!' he snivelled. 'He should never have given it to a Falzard! What did he expect?' He fell silent for a few seconds and composed himself. *Not even my parents wanted me* he thought, remembering the orphanage.

'There is one person who may be able to help us,' said the wand.

'Us?' Fizbar laughed at the reference, 'And who would that be?'

'Gildor.'

Fizbar chose to say nothing and gave a non-committal shake of his head. Instead he began to walk in the direction that would lead him towards the home of his old teacher.

11

The Magic Garden

Fizbar felt the aftermath of the sun on the back of his neck; it was sore. He had been out for most of the day and he now welcomed the cool evening hours. As the sun set in the west he approached one of Sintar's many alleys that would lead him to the shop of Helena Elantiel, Wizard of the Fourth Order and Master of Potions. He thought back to the journal Therolius had given him. Therolius hadn't said much about it. What was it for? Why did he give it to me? With all these unanswered questions floating around with no answers to greet them he came to a black door with two large red ribbons that hung on either side from iron rails. He looked up and read the yellow sign with its green leafy lettering *The Magic Garden*. He turned the door handle until he heard a click, and then entered.

A tiny bell rang from above the door. The shop was brand new and the smell of fresh paint tickled the tip of Fizbar's nose. He sneezed. Large shelves filled the room and towered into nowhere. Fizbar looked up and couldn't see the end of the spiralling ladder that ran alongside them. The shop was small from the outside, but inside was taller than any shop in Sintar; even taller than castles and council buildings. It was the source of many plants and potions for wizards, even those who were more than capable of making potions themselves. Herbology had become something of a local interest in Sintar. It was a harmonious and happy relationship that suited everyone, whilst many like Helena profited.

The shop was full of people. Not only wizards and herbalist's frequented the shop, anybody with an affection for plants was welcome. Plants graced the shop in different colours although they were predominately green. Small ones, large ones and even giants ones. Big leaf, broad leaf, small leaf, and tiny leaves. Even dried up trees with crooked branches stood tall, gracing the corners. Many jars and containers packed the shop. Some closed, others open, and many arranged in neat rows on the shelves below and high above. Four large containers were filled to the brim with strange green and muddy goo. They sat on the ground next to the shop display window. In the goo were giant swamp plants that danced; their leafy stalks curling in the air. They were all swaying, but Fizbar hoped they were harmless and posed him no threat. To be sure he made a face at them. They replied with a large raspberry; strange flowery buds shot beautiful tongues at him, which then fanned open before closing tightly. As they shot some goo at his eyes he stumbled and fell backwards over a large empty pot, pulling out his wand at the same time. He knocked the table and small jars fell crashing on the floor. On a table next to him was a gyrating jar, which was ready to fall on Fizbar's head. Everybody noticed his entrance and Helena quickly left the comfort of her guests to hurry towards him, trying to prevent more jars from falling off the displays she had painstakingly prepared.

Fizbar got up and hit his head on the table, knocking a wooden cane that rolled off to one side. It hit a series of tall hollow glass flutes that sat next to the shop counter half-filled with earth, and like dominoes they fell one after the other. Suddenly the air was filled with the sound of glass crashing on the floor. Fizbar quickly directed his wand to the crashing sounds and whispered thinking nobody would notice, '*Adhaeresco*,' but as he tried to pronounce it the gyrating jar fell and hit him on the head causing him to redirect his wand towards the swamp plants. A green waft of light left the end of his spoon and hit the plants.

'*Oh dear*,' whispered his wand. '*This doesn't look good.*'

At that point Fizbar curled his bottom lip quickly and popped the wand into his pocket. Everyone in the shop immediately stopped what they were doing and stared at the falling glass with their mouths wide-open. The swamp plants began shooting goo in every direction. The plants fired a sticky substance towards the guests and some of them raised their arms to guard their faces from the projectile slime.

Helena narrowed her delicate brow. She had noticed that Fizbar had not spoken a spell the second time. She shrugged it off so she could tend to the situation at hand. Fizbar crawled over to the counter and hid under it, hoping that it would ease the pain to his ears as well as to his ego. More jars fell to the floor and Fizbar jumped at every crash. He was already thinking about his likely fate and Helena's reaction. Goo flew in every direction. Helena took a deep breath and shaking her hand brought out her wand. It was a beech wand which became animated, coiling around her hand until it stopped at her index finger straightening it as if she was ready to point at something.

'... *Positus!*' shouted Helena finally as she pointed her wand at the falling jars, containers, plants and anything else that was out of place. As her wand arm swung around her body everything slowly rewound until they were back in their place. She quickly pointed to the last remaining shards of glass. '*Sarcio positus!*' she hailed. The jars flickered in the light as they began to paste themselves together, whilst returning to their original places. Fizbar crawled out of his refuge and along the floor before getting up and rubbing his head behind a couple of taller strangers who blocked his view.

'Fine entrance, Fizbar!' his wand declared. He felt the comment didn't deserve an answer, and he felt embarrassed.

When it was all over everyone clapped at Helena's performance. Fizbar walked to the front of the crowd clapping, acting as though it wasn't his fault. Helena and the crowd shot him looks of disdain, shaking their heads. Helena returned to her guests. Fizbar noticed his old history teacher Gildor prowling among the shelves, grunting and purring as he caught sight of familiar plants and ingredients. He obviously wasn't upset by Fizbar's actions. The chatter resumed and regained its former noisy level.

'I believe you had the right spell master, what went wrong?' asked the wand tactfully.

Fizbar noticed Therolius in a far corner unmoved by the commotion and talking to Gimera. They seemed to be having a disagreement of some sort and Gimera stormed off in a temper.

'A jar hit me on the head.'

'Oh I see, but it still hasn't knocked any sense into you has it?'

'Less of the lip,' Fizbar snapped.

'I mean if your spell was right, what went wrong?'

'It must have hit the swamp plants.'

'Oh, I see now. I guess they started firing their green goo at everything and everyone.'

'You know me well,' said Fizbar, with half a smile.

'I'm your wand, Master, I have got used to the outcomes of your spell casting. Don't you for one minute think that I channel all your magic. Which brings me to my next question. What happened to the second spell?'

'What second spell?'

'The one that caused all the unruly behaviour.'

'I don't know what you mean,' he said concerned, but still feeling sorry for himself. 'No spell came out of you. I have no idea what you're on about.'

'Every wizard is graced with unique potential, but I felt something… Strange.'

'Yeah, so did I.'

'I hope you're not keeping anything from me,' said Fizbar.

'Why do you say that?'

'I don't know, but I need to find out.'

Fizbar looked towards the Overlord. Surely he would have the answers. As he approached him he saw a concerned look on the Overlord's face. He was halfway across the floor when a girl blocked his path. She stared at him openly, sipping a drink. He brushed past her, knocking her slightly to one side, without apologising. He continued towards Therolius.

'A sorry would be nice,' said the girl in a slightly nettled tone. He turned to face her. She was wiping the drink from her blouse with a tissue.

'Excuse me, err…sorry, but I need to see Thero—'

'Your entrance was remarkable,' she said. 'I've never seen Helena use her wand. She says dealing with plants requires very little use of a wand, but I know that's not the main reason.' The girl's face was glazed and pale. Her long brown hair fell to her shoulders. A kink suggested she kept it in a ponytail. Her grey eyes were striking and stood out from her pallid complexion. She wore a white blouse with a thin black belt across her waist. A patterned burgundy tweed skirt fell just below her knees. It fitted her perfectly and tightly like a schoolgirl. Black finger nail polish didn't match her outfit. It was odd, but Fizbar didn't think anything of it.

'I don't mean to be rude, but what are you talking about?' said Fizbar as his head darted back in the direction of the Overlord, who had now vanished from view.

'I'm actually glad she's using it again,' the girl said in an eloquent voice. 'No, in fact I'm really glad she's using it again. Helena's very secretive when it comes to her wand. Says a wand is more like a private quest, whatever that means.' She threw the soiled tissue into a nearby bin.

Fizbar could only stare. 'Us wizards,' he pointed to himself, 'are very secretive when it comes to our wands.' He finished with a whisper whilst studying the girl from head to toe.

'Do you come to this store often?' asked the girl, her eyelashes fluttering.

'Quite a lot actually, to get what I need for my potions.

Unlike other wizards who are lazy and just buy the bottled stuff.' He cupped his hands around his mouth and raised his voice a little so some of the other wizards heard him.

The girl giggled.

'Just usually in a quieter way.' He looked at her blouse. 'I really am sorry about that.'

'Don't worry. I have a good potion that will remove the stain.'

'I'm actually working on a healing potion myself,' said Fizbar, sure of himself and oozing confidence, 'but it's rather laborious work,' he lied.

'You are a wizard then!' she jested, staring at Fizbar's hat and his robe. Slightly bashful, she giggled again like a shy girl. She was sweet. He laughed casually; he thought it would be impolite not to.

'I'm a little clumsy at times,' he admitted.

'I would never have guessed.'

They both laughed.

'I've seen you in the paper if I remember correctly.' She scratched her right temple, trying to recall. 'Ah yes, something about a terrorising dragon?'

She waited for a reply.

'I got the job done, that's the main thing,' Fizbar grunted, 'very few wizards would confront a dragon. They possess the old magic and a lot of fire. I suppose us newly qualified ones are less afraid of a challenge. Less fear of the unknown,' he smirked.

A slight crimson glow appeared on her cheeks.

'Can I get you another drink? Seems proper as I spilt your first one,' he said already picking up a cup of orange liquid and handing it to her. It fell to the floor. 'Butter fingers,' said Fizbar. He picked up another with a tighter grip and handed it to her.

'I love plant juice. Especially, *Arnebia densiflora*. It's actually very good for your bowels.' Fizbar peeked at the table from the corner of his eye, and then back to his cup without moving his head. 'Well…' He realised this was the table that Helena was using for her samples to promote her business, and felt foolish. 'Hmm,' he nodded.

She tightened her lips to prevent a laugh, and then looked down at the floor to avoid the bewildered look on his face.

'But you already knew that didn't you?' she said with a smile showing her perfect teeth.

'Yes.' He sprang with the answer. He lied; he didn't have a clue what it was.

'That's why I'm working on this healing potion.'

She bit her lip. A tingle raised the hairs on the back of Fizbar's neck.

'Are you new in Sintar?'

'No. Not really. I left Sintar to study in Fintar almost six years ago, but I'm back now. I'm a Herbalistic Potions Master. I graduated last month.'

'Wow! Congratulations! A herbalist! Do you know

that I excelled at the school of magic in herbology?' He lied again. 'Although I remember my teacher telling me quite the opposite. Something to do with eating the wrong mushrooms,' he added truthfully.

'It's not easy, and it takes a lot of patience as well as dedication to knowing the plants – pure hard work! People think it's easy, but that's their downfall. I never had the aptitude for magic like my mother and I definitely wasn't a blue-blood. I was lucky that I was good at what I loved. So I opted to study herbology at the Fintar School of Botany.'

Fizbar was transfixed. The girl put her cup down and opened her hand.

'Hetty by the way.'

'Sorry?' said Fizbar.

'My name… It's Hetty.'

Fizbar leapt forward and shook her hand vigorously. 'Fizbar, Fizbar Trundle.'

'Pleased to meet you Fizbar Trundle. And your wand? It's only fair I meet him or her.'

'Thurrock! He's male, although he acts like a female from time-to-time. But he's been quiet for a while.'

The wand tried to speak, but Fizbar immediately clenched his pocket; only muffled sounds emanated. He felt edgy and antsy. He felt ashamed that his wand was a spoon. He didn't want to reveal himself as a Falzard, not just yet anyway, and especially not to a girl.

'Can I see it?'

'See what?'

'Your wand, silly.'

He thought hard. He wanted to show her, but he had only just met her. Although there was something about her that was different from other girls, he didn't know her well enough to confide in her. He couldn't. He was sure she'd find out soon enough anyway, that's if she had read the whole article in the paper, or had seen his wand during his epic entrance.

'Why don't you tell me more about Fintar first? Is it as green as they say? I've always wanted to go. I missed an outing there when I was at magic school. Mr Zackus our head of year said it was a once in a lifetime opportunity.'

Fizbar picked Mr Zackus out of the crowd and waved. His black-rimmed glasses seemed bigger than his face but his large bushy hair made them look normal. Gildor Zackus replied with a bemused half-wave.

'I found out it was because the school didn't get any more funding for further trips. They put all the money into the tenderfoots these days, little consideration for the apprentices.' He diverted from the subject regaining his breath. She was a little curious and puzzled. She still wondered about his wand, but she decided not to persist any further.

'It's lovely,' she replied. Hetty looked him in straight in the eye. She found him a little odd, though interesting.

'My mother always said that she would have moved to Fintar if it hadn't been for her having a sweetheart.'

'Yes you were saying. Your mother is a wizard? Does she live here in Sintar?' He scratched his nose.

She nodded with a foolish smile.

'Do I know her?' He put one hand on the table and with the other he touched his waist. He looked like a teapot.

She nodded again. 'You should if you shop here often. She owns this place,' said Hetty with open arms.

Fizbar's eyebrows rose and he could feel the strain on his forehead. 'Medra! The farrier's wife?'

'Not her, not the help.'

Fizbar thought harder and Hetty sniggered like a little girl. She pointed towards the crowd and a woman with a hard look on her face glanced their way.

'Helena? *She's* your mother?' he said.

'Yes,' replied Hetty with a large half-moon smile.

'Is your mother here Fizbar?' She panned around the room from left to right scanning the heads, 'Your father?' she added.

'No. Neither are here… It's just me.' He felt a little sad, and a feeling of emptiness also crept in.

'Are they at home?'

'No, nobody at home except me.'

'And your wand.' Then Hetty giggled.

Fizbar managed a smile, pointing to her as if to say, "you got me".

Hetty didn't know whether to pursue it any further, but before she could decide Fizbar did it for her.

'My father ran away and my mother died giving birth to me.' He fiddled with his goatee, his eyes following the tiles on the floor.' At least that's what Therolius told me.'

'Oh.' She didn't know how to react or what to say. 'Did he know them well?'

'I'm not sure. He never told me much. He picked me up from the orphanage and brought me to the school. That's all I know.'

'Oh.' Hetty still didn't know how to respond. '… Therolius seems, somewhat sad.'

'I think he continues to live with the guilt of what happened to Zalbar all those years ago. What he did to him as a tenderfoot I mean, you know the story. Always in the clouds, absent minded and…'

'Just very sad,' Hetty cut in.

'Yes, I suppose so.'

'My friends in Fintar say the Lex Talionis are starting to be become problematic. Crime continues to increase, but not as much as here, not at the moment that is. They seem more powerful here. Word on the street is that Zalbar is here. There is a high percentage of truth in rumours you know.'

Fizbar's eyes widened as he thought back to the book. He pulled her close to a corner where long curtains hung. Away from prying eyes and big ears.

'Zalbar's here?' She nodded.

'Where? Do you know?' he asked with interest.

'Not sure. Like I said, there are a lot of unsubstantiated rumours. There have been numerous Lex sightings in Fintar Forest.'

'That's odd,' he said, remembering. 'My last job was in that area and a hunchback told me that his master was in the Lex Talionis. When I told Therolius he said he was Zalbar's hunchback.'

She looked on in amazement. 'Zalbar's hunchback!' she repeated in a high-pitched whisper.

Fizbar nodded, but urged her to keep her voice down.

'*Thank goodness the Overlord is close by,*' Hetty whispered.

He nodded. 'It's odd because he gave me something yesterday. He seemed really nervous about something. Worried in fact.' Fizbar tapped his left pocked with his right hand. His head was fixed on the crowd. He looked back at Hetty.

'What was it?'

He thought he'd talked too much already. 'Just an empty journal.' Fizbar wanted to show her, but Therolius's presence reminded him that he would be breaking his promise.

'Oh, that is odd. An empty journal?' she said. 'Maybe it was a gift so you could start creative writing.'

The shop was now full of people. The swamp plants

became the centre of attention and danced to entertain a group of wizards. They blew lots of raspberries. She noticed a green stain on the wooden unit next to the plants and used her sleeve to remove it before she made her way to the main desk.

'I don't think this journal is for writing in.'

'Why not?' asked Hetty.

Three knocks came from the desk where Therolius held a large wooden hammer. He looked like a judge about to pass sentence. He started to address the people in the shop, with Helena by his side. Fizbar and Hetty listened to the Overlord formally opening the new shop. Hetty picked up her drink and took a sip. She grabbed Fizbar's hand, urging him to follow her closer to the front. He followed her, still feeling that tingle, but didn't answer her earlier question. How could he tell her the journal belonged to Geldahar Zalbar, the enemy?

12

Gildor's Shack

Gildor didn't exactly live in a palace; it was far from regal. The small house was in fact a shack, and almost in the middle of nowhere. Gildor lived just ten minutes from the centre of Sintar, but a large field separated him from the populace. Only two large trees stood firm and close as if guarding the wizard's house. The nearby river crept from the north and swirled further south until it vanished out of sight and underground. Fizbar walked across the grassy terrain annoyed at the mud that clung to his shoes making his feet heavy to lift out of the squishy ground. His toes were cold, but warm thoughts about Hetty soon distracted him from his discomfort. He simply couldn't wait to see her again.

Tall grass brushed against his cloak, wetting it, turning it a darker shade. The morning's crisp air mixed with the warmth of his breath created little humid clouds like a steam train. As he trampled up to the house he suddenly hit something and fell to the ground. His knees were now wet and he quickly lifted himself from the grassy loam rubbing his nose and wiping himself with his other hand at the same time. Strange white lights danced around as if electricity were visible. Then they slowly fizzled from sight.

'Hoowissit?' A loud voice in a strange, wiry accent sprang from the air, with a short-lived echo.

Fizbar looked up and around, turning, trying to locate the source and looking dumbfounded. 'Err... Fizbar,' he replied. His eyes rolled up, as if he were addressing the Gods.

'And what do ya want?'

'I need to see Gildor. It's important.'

There was a slight pause. Then the voice returned. 'On da count a three, jump forwards. Starting... Na!'

Fizbar didn't have time to think and leapt forward almost immediately. A subtle electronic sound buzzed twice; then silence.

'Up ya come then.'

Fizbar walked toward the door inspecting the little shack from the base upwards. He touched the panels with outstretched hands; feeling the wooden grain and attempting to locate the entrance. It was a small house if you could call it a house at all. It was about six metres high and the four wooden grey walls all looked the same. A much larger addition to the building that looked like an extension stretched from the back of the shack and seemed never ending. The T-shaped building had small individual doors that ran along a lengthy exterior just like cat flaps, but were fastened shut with strips of wood and plenty of nails; it looked derelict.

With both hands flat out on an area of wood Fizbar knocked with a *rat-a-tat-tat* and a door appeared in front of him. As it opened he looked down at a small figure with a large nose and chin and head shaped like a white skinned potato. His bald head looked like the top end of an egg and white hair sat on either side just below the temples; just above his large pointed ears. Small round spectacles looked stupid on him, as his eyes were much larger than the lenses. It was a Clurichaun.

'You're a Leprechaun.'

'And ya'd be sorta right! Your eyes serve you well, unlike mine.' He squinted, and then hiccupped. 'Come in and sit down. Gildor will be with ya in a moment.'

Fizbar entered and took off his wizard's hat. He examined the room which appeared very homely and sophisticated, unlike its outer barn-like appearance. It was considerably larger on the inside than it was on the outside. The shell seemed like a disused shed, but on the inside it was more like a mansion. They were in a circular room fitted with veneer bookcases that were filled with different coloured hardback books. An Anatolian carpet full of lively colours covered the middle of the floor. Vibrant yellows and reds leapt from within a thick black frame, which looked as if safeguarding the energy. Fizbar walked over to a small riveted burgundy and velvet chair. He sat down continuing to inspect his surroundings. A portable cast iron fireplace sat in the middle of the circular room. A half-pint tin kettle sat on the smaller of two hotplates and it was starting to whistle softly.

'Ah! Fizbar. How nice it is to see an old student of mine. How are you, dear boy?' Gildor appeared, beside him a large white cat that resembled a miniature panther walked gracefully; purring loudly. Fizbar's eyes bulged. Gildor noticed the unease in Fizbar's reaction, so he bent over and rubbed the cat's furry neck down to her belly.

'She's a Granther, a cross between a Grimalkin and a White Mountain panther. Beautiful creature, aren't you my lovely, yes you are.' Gildor stroked her head affectionately. 'I have more in the farmhouse. I breed them when I'm not teaching at the school. Lovely magical creatures and don't worry Fizbar, Keldra wouldn't harm a soul. Would you girl?'

'Unless ya told her to!' said the leprechaun. He hiccupped.

The cat followed Gildor with her flickering, piercing yellow eyes fixed on Fizbar.

'I see you've met Bran.'

'Yes, he speaks a little strangely.'

'I know. He's from a place called sub-Ireland. Never

heard of it myself. He says it's "beyond the seas of seas".'
He made his way to a chair opposite to Fizbar and sat
down letting out a small bellow. Keldra followed her
master with a snarly hiss, and then curled at his feet.

'I found Bran by the river one day entwined in a fishing
line singing strange tunes. He told me he got here on an
inflatable chair. All I knew was that he hadn't caught any
fish and the river was littered with hundreds of empty
green bottles.'

'Fine wine it was... Fine wine.' Bran licked the lips
of his wide mouth, smiled and entered a daydream. He
hiccupped again.

'I'd rather have a tea if you don't mind.' Gildor pointed
to the kettle that was now whistling wildly. 'I'm sure
Fizbar wouldn't mind a cup?'

Bran snarled and walked over to the stove mumbling.
He poured two cups and handed one to Fizbar who thanked
him and one to Gildor, who didn't. Bran wiped his hands
on a brown apron that fell to his knees; then broke into
song accompanied by a hiccup as he left the room.

Gildor smiled and then took a sip of his tea. 'So Fizbar,
what is so important? I imagine your visit is not purely
social.' His button-like face was small and his eyes seemed
smaller hidden behind his glasses. The hair that was left
on his head was sparse and seemed to be moving as well
as standing on end. His tweed suit was primarily red tartan
with prominent black lines. His purple tie looked odd and

certainly out of place.

Fizbar pulled the journal from his pocket and stared at it before handing it over to Gildor, who coughed. His demeanour changed almost instantly.

'Sorry, a little tea went down the wrong hole. May I ask where you got that?' he enquired with a shiver.

'Therolius gave it to me,' said Fizbar.

Gildor read the lettering on the front of *The Binding Journal* and sank deeper into his chair. 'Why would he do that?'

'I was hoping you could answer that for me. He didn't say much. It's evident a lot of his actions are still clouded by the Zalbar guilt, pointless really, as it was all a long time ago and not his fault.'

He registered Gildor's anxiety, but took another sip of his tea. 'Therolius told me he wants me to keep it safe,' he added.

There was a short pause.

'You know what this is don't you, Gildor?' he asked. 'I can see it on your face.'

'It's easy to piece it together if you have the right information.'

Gildor stared blankly over the rim of his cup. He drank his tea down in one gulp, closing his eyes, pondering on what to say next. Then he placed the cup and saucer on a small table that was next to his chair. The rattling cup made Kelda's head pop up and her ears point to the ceiling like radars.

'It's a binding journal belonging to Geldahar Zalbar. But why give it to me? I don't want it.'

Gildor waited for a response. Instead, he raised his hands and shrugged his shoulders. He had no answer. Or did he? He pointed directly at the journal. 'What has Therolius told you about this?'

'Like I said, nothing. Only to keep it safe, and not to open it.'

'And I bet you've opened it.' He hoped the answer would be denial. There was a painful pause.

'Just for a few seconds… It fell out of my pocket, but I managed to shut it almost immediately.'

'Huh!' said his wand.

Fizbar knew Gildor didn't believe him as evidenced by his reaction and flustered face. 'Didn't you listen to the Overlord? He wouldn't tell you something just for the sake of it.'

'But…'

'I'm afraid the damage is already done.'

'What damage?'

'The damage you have created by opening Zalbar's journal.'

'What could possibly happen from opening a book?' Fizbar asked, tired of all the guessing games. 'I did it all the time at school, people do it all the time; everyday.'

'But not book is like this one. Thanks to your actions

Zalbar now knows where the journal is.'

'What do you mean? The pages were blank; I saw it with my own eyes. What's the point of an empty journal?'

'It doesn't make any difference, Fizbar. Zalbar will come for it. This is a binding journal and is also bound to the wizard's magical channel. As soon as you opened it the magic it possesses sent a message to Zalbar's wand. It's like a lost and found mechanism.' Gildor lifted himself out of the chair and began pacing frantically up and down. The white cat followed, mimicking the actions of her master. 'You must leave, Fizbar, it's not safe anymore. The Lex could be here any minute.' He looked around, surveying each wall and the ceiling. 'It's only a matter of time before they track you down. You need to leave here, now.'

'Gildor, you have a magical force field out there.' Fizbar pointed behind him without turning his body. 'I couldn't get through without Bran, so we should be safe here.'

'Oh no… Bran had to disenchant the field in order to let you through. Anyone could have got through when you did.' His pacing was making Fizbar dizzy and anxious. Kelda was also becoming restless, her purring had stopped and a low growl rumbled from her belly. Gildor muttered, wiping his forehead. '*Oh Feena… Feena.*'

'That's my mother's name. Why are you mentioning her name?' Fizbar's voice broke for a moment but his eyes widened with intrigue.

'Your mother was a kind woman. A pure spirit… But she was, corrupted.'

'How would you know? You didn't even know her? I didn't even know her.' Fizbar paused. 'Did you… Know her?' Fizbar asked again, this time demanding an answer.

Gildor faced the fireplace, away from Fizbar, both hands on the mantelpiece. He gestured with a slow nod. 'I had the ultimate adoration for your mother, but the feeling wasn't mutual. Her affection lay with someone else.'

'My father… Jack.'

Gildor didn't reply, but his expression suggested he was hiding something. The sweat began trickling down his button-like face. He wasn't sure how much time he had.

'What are you hiding, Gildor?'

Again he chose not to answer. He shook his head repeatedly as though trying to remove demons from inside it. The cat became even more agitated and she sniffed the air.

'Zalbar… He didn't deserve her. None of them did… Gimera. I knew you'd…' He muttered like a confused man. The cat roared a few times. Gildor took some deep breaths trying to calm himself, but the Granther became even more restless. Bran ran in wondering why the animal was roaring before focusing on Gildor who raised his oak wand. Then out of nowhere two large black smoky animals appeared in the room. The roars were louder than

Kelda's who was now roaring and hissing. They took the form of large black bears with short faces, menacing teeth and glowing red eyes.

'ARCTODI!' shouted Gildor whose wand was at the ready. The wand made Fizbar feel comfort in his own. He noticed the oak wand had brown tape wrapped around the handle. But Fizbar's comfort was soon extinguished when he also noticed another three black and smokey figures appearing in the room. For now the thought of his parents and Gildor's poor explanation were pushed to the back of his mind.

'LEX TALIONIS!' shouted Gildor. 'RUN FIZBAR RUN! GET OUT OF HERE! GO TO NIMVAR AT THE GROVE. HE'LL KNOW WHAT TO DO!' His voice was only just audible, muffled by animal roars. Gildor released shards of coloured light from his wand, which hit the bears, preventing them from fully taking form. Kelda started to glow, a faint yellow aura exuded from her white coat as she pounced at one of the bears. The bears' teeth dripped with saliva and their long talons looked as though they ached to rip flesh. For the moment ripping books seemed to suffice, and they tore the pages with ease. Bran ran in with two empty wine bottles and started waving them fiercely in the air at the bear Gildor was tackling. It ignored him, kicking him over and knocking him flying with its hind paw back in the direction he had come. Fizbar ran out the door not looking back and three half-formed figures ran after him.

'STOP HIM, GET THE BOOK!' shouted one with an eye patch. His clothes were frayed and filthy.

As Fizbar ran along the field he tripped over a rock, and landed facing his pursuers. One of them was chubby. His head rounded with two fat cheeks and a small red nose that matched the size of his button-like eyes. He didn't look menacing, but his smoky aura did. The other one had an eye patch and drew a long crow's feather from his tattered pocket. The chubby one drew a gold pen. The last of the smoke and liquid strands had vanished and they were fully formed. They approached Fizbar across the last few yards, slowly and in a threatening manner. The chubby man snarled like a dog. Fizbar dipped into his pocket for his wand. The one with the eye patch tutted, swaying his feather. 'I wouldn't do that if I was you... Leave the spoon alone.'

'What do you want with me?' Fizbar asked breathing heavily; his heart pounding like a drum.

'That little journal you've got in your pocket will do nicely; then we can all go home and have a nice cup of tea.'

'Yeah! We know you have it. Come on! Hand it over,' said the chubby man seemingly in a hurry.

'I don't know what you're...'

'DON'T play stupid with me, little Falzard,' said Viktor, scowling.

'I'm not a Falzard, so I would be careful with your accusations.'

Both the men giggled as if they had heard the greatest joke ever told.

'Then hand it over,' said the chubby man. 'Ain't that right, Badger?' He chuckled.

Viktor turned to him, his facial gestures indicating he'd acted like an imbecile. Viktor then turned around and reached out. Fizbar kicked his feet forwards pushing himself back a little and without hurrying dipped his hand into his pocket. There was something more to this journal. More than Therolius had told him or even prepared him for. The brown leather journal was poking from his pocket; he gripped it firmly with his sweaty hand.

'There, that's better. A little more and over here,' said Viktor waving towards him, 'nice and slow and don't get any clever ideas.'

Fizbar didn't have any clever ideas, in fact he couldn't even think of a spell. 'I've heard of you. You're The Badger.' He pointed to the streak of white hair whilst staggering to his feet. His eyes became relaxed and he was ready to admit defeat until he noticed a faint flicker of colour in the background.

'That'll be right. My reputation shadows me.' He tried a courteous bow, but only half-succeeded with it. His eyes were fixed on Fizbar's hand and the journal.

'I don't like this,' whispered his wand.

'There's something behind you,' said Fizbar, lifting his head.

Viktor chuckled.

'The oldest trick in the book. Is that the best you can do?' said the chubby smoke demon.

'What are you playing at?' asked the spoon.

Fizbar shushed his wand and raised a hand, guarding his eyes from a bright ray of light as the sun passed from cloud to cloud. The other hand still clutched the journal. The sun was battling with the clouds and it was difficult to see without opening your eyes wide. A cloud passed, blocking the sun and allowing more shaded time. Another light, this time green, appeared from the shack and seemed to be travelling faster. Both lights grew closer and closer. Yet the Lex Talionis were still unaware.

'WHAT ARE YOU WAITING FOR?' shouted Viktor, saliva launching from his unhygienic mouth. 'Hand it over NOW!'

The chubby man chortled, with a nasal snort. Fizbar bent his knees and got up steadily. He paced towards the Badger until the book was inches from Viktor's tattered, gloved hand. Viktor's eyes fixed on the journal, watery, yet burning with determination. He hesitated for a second, wetting his lips, poised to grab the book.

As a thick cloud overhead darkened the sky, Viktor looked up and noticed a rainbow of colours dance on Fizbar's pale face. Viktor plummeted forward almost immediately puffing into a liquidy cloud as a Granther pounced on him. Fizbar jerked to one side avoiding any contact whilst shoving the book back in his pocket at the same time. The other Granther had managed to get there in the nick of time and tore at the chubby man. But he too, like Viktor, vanished into thin air, leaving only black, smoky strands dancing against the now blue and cotton wool sky. Fizbar welcomed the rescue and narrowed his eyes at the distance between him and the shack in hope of spotting Gildor. He wanted to go back, but knew Gildor would disapprove. Instead he lowered his hands and turned to the Granthers.

'Thanks Kelda,' he said to the one with yellow eyes. Then he approached the other drawn to its radiant blue eyes. The cat shuffled backwards with hesitancy; then it hissed. Fizbar behaved carefully. He didn't want to agitate or annoy the large cat, so he chose to stand still.

Both cats howled and as they did, their eyes glowed brightly. Then they raced away back to the shack. Fizbar quivered at the cold breeze as the thick cloud cleared. He hoped Gildor was all right.

13

The Grove

With a burst of light Fizbar appeared, a little wobbly and balancing on one foot, on top of a large grey boulder that poked from the ground.

'Told you it would work,' said his wand confidently.

'Yes, but we didn't land in the grove did we?' replied Fizbar.

'I do remember saying that there's no spell for that part of the forest. It's either at the entrance or farther from the rear.'

'Remind me to throw one together when we get back to include everything else.'

'There's a little more to it than simply throwing a spell together. Do remember that only—'

'Yes, I know! Only a highly skilled spell-caster has the ability to create spells of magnitude.' Fizbar made a face, which threw him off balance. He waved his hands and arms frantically like a flightless bird before falling off the boulder and rolling; somehow managing to get back to his feet.

'That'll teach you. And also there's a reason no spells have been made for this part,' said his wand.

'Hunchbacks?'

'Precisely.'

'I guess we'll have to trek the remainder on foot then, won't we, dear spoon?'

'And there's no need for sarcasm…'

After half a morning's trek up a dirty and dusty track towards the forest entrance, Fizbar's head began to throb. He felt giddy and light headed as blood pumped fiercely through the veins along the sides of his face. He could hear the amplified beats of his own heart as the sound grew in intensity, seeming to occur next to his ears. He crouched and took some deep, calming breaths. Then as if a shard of ice had pierced his brain he shut his eyes. Flickers of many unfamiliar faces taunted him. Some faces he knew, but they were emotionless. Scenes and visions of hunchbacks thrusting torches high in the air and shouting in anger were very vivid. It was so realistic that he felt he was there, walking amongst them. They even looked down at him with hostile stares, and expressions of revulsion. Kneeling down amongst the commotion he looked up, then slowly the view panned upwards until he saw what looked like an sacrificial altar surrounded by candles with orange flames that looked like stars. The hunchbacks circled the altar, leaving ample space for a body that lay upon it. The view then zoomed in fast, like a bullet, but left him with a glimpse, an imprint of the Therolius's face. The Overlord was troubled, still and expressionless. Then just as quickly as they had come, the visions disappeared. Fizbar noticed that he had bitten his lip, and touching with a finger he felt a little blood. It wasn't really painful, just sore.

'What was that…?' said Fizbar, his hands bracing his head. After a long pause, he said, 'Did…'

'Yes, I felt something too.' His wand replied. 'Strange.'

'I saw faces… Some sort of vision. It was full of hunchbacks shouting or chanting or something.' His cold hands ran down to soothe his eyes; giving temporary relief.

'You've been working hard lately. Taking on too many jobs. First the dragon, followed by the hunchback. Or maybe you're straining your eyes and need glasses. That can cause headaches and visions.'

'Maybe. But this wasn't any ordinary headache. It was strange, and I felt… Helpless, like I was there.' He rose to his feet again, a little unsteady, then he said: 'The hunchbacks. There must be a reason why I'm seeing them.'

'Maybe Nimvar can explain.' The wand's tone was unconvincing.

'Maybe you're right.' Fizbar straightened his back and

stretched his legs before carrying on. He checked his cloak pocket for the journal to see if it was still there. He smiled when he established it was.

The day was pleasant and a light breeze moved the trees of the grove. It was full of fruit trees bearing fruit of different shapes, colours and sizes. The mixed bouquet of fragrances was sweet as well as mouth-watering. Fizbar's tummy began to rumble. He continued to walk down a grassy and pebble-strewn path that added a light spring to his step. The grove was a cultivated area, man-made, or at least something made. As they approached a towering bare root hedge he spotted a door-like shape carved in it. He continued cautiously through the vivid green wall and to his astonishment a large dome-like structure of rock appeared in front of him. It was a gigantic boulder, much bigger than the one he had landed on. In fact it was the biggest he had ever seen. It made Gildor's shack look like a toy shed. Ahead of him was the cave opening. Fizbar walked a few paces and couldn't help but stare at the structure. It was entwined by thick roots the size of tree trunks. The pine tree roots coiled around the boulder like a snake constricting its prey. It looked natural but Fizbar wondered if a wizard had had something to do with its creation. The intricate coils of Mother Nature, the way both stone and flora graced each other, Fizbar thought, *That's what I call real magic*. The entrance to the cave was dank, chilly and gave off a pungent odour. He looked to the floor and noticed trails of gooey saliva amongst many footprints, evidence that this passage was used a lot and that someone or something lived here. A little help from his wand and some starlight lit up the darkness. A shiver ran down Fizbar's spine; the chilled and hollow surrounding amplified his unease.

'What do you suppose is in here?' Fizbar asked.

His wand was silent.

'You've been quiet for a while. Anything wrong?'

A pause and then, 'No.'

Fizbar wasn't entirely satisfied with the reply, but the situation removed any need to converse.

They finally came to a forked tunnel. Two forks in one direction and two in another. Fizbar pondered for a moment before picking the largest opening, but he decided to tread carefully and with his wand at the ready. He lifted his wand slightly to redirect the light when a large hand appeared from above his head and grabbed the spoon. Fizbar felt immense strength, but didn't let go as the hand pulled both him and his wand upwards into the air. It only took a little wiggle of the wand for Fizbar to lose his grip and fall to the floor.

'Grab the spoon!' said a deep growling voice, 'and I'll grab 'im.'

Before Fizbar could see who had spoken, a larger hand

grabbed him pulling him up quickly and thrusting his lanky body over a very large shoulder, but he managed to roll off to the floor. He felt the wind on his face, but the chamber was dark and he could barely see. A hand advanced to his neck and he got a glimpse of what was in front of him. The grip was tight and painful. He couldn't turn his head and his eyes felt like they were about to pop out of their sockets, but thankfully he could still breathe.

After a few minutes journey a large club-fingered hand swung the wizard around. In front of him were two large, mean, scruffy looking hunchbacks. They were dressed in scattered metal armour plates. One of the hunchback's eyes were so narrowed that it appeared he had no eyes at all, just a large bushy and protruding forehead. The other's eyes were large like plums. Between them they had enough hair to cover just one of their heads, but they were huge. Both wore green undergarments that were mottled brown. The narrow-eyed one carried a large spiked mace. Fizbar peered down at it. He was hanging in the air supported by his neck. He managed to swallow hard and felt the veins pumping in his head. Plum Eyes handed Fizbar's wand to Narrow Eyes; at the same time Fizbar dropped to the floor. He touched his neck and felt the bruised areas where the strong fingers had dug into him. He chose not to turn to see what was happening. He hoped he wouldn't be hoisted up again.

'A wizard 'ere. How'd he get 'ere?' said Narrow Eyes

who grabbed him again by the neck.

'Lots of wizards know we're 'ere. Especially, the Order of Light. Maybe we should eat 'im,' said Plum Eyes.

'Hmmm! I can smell it already.' Narrow Eyes rubbed his nose against Fizbar from his waist up to his shoulder, leaving a trail of mucous.

Fizbar's face exuded disgust, retching at the smell before focusing back on the pain in his neck. The hunchbacks grunted with a hint of laughter. Fizbar's eyes couldn't help but dart from one to the other. The grip was just as hard as the previous time and his neck began to throb through the numbness. The hunchbacks continued chatting amongst themselves.

'Yes... Order of Light...' Fizbar strained to release the words. He thought about what to say next.

'Whatcha doing 'ere then?' said Narrow Eyes, centimetres from the wizard's nose. 'Who sent you?' Mucous dripped from his nose.

'Sent... By Gildor... To see Nimvar,' he whispered.

The hunchback grunted. Plum Eyes scratched his head, and then wiped away the mucous that had been trickling down his large nostrils onto his torso. The hunchbacks looked at each other in dismay and shrugged their shoulders. Fizbar felt the journal slipping from his pocket as they walked into a room filled with hunchbacks. It looked like a festive hall and a party was already in full swing. Rotten food lay extensively along seemingly never-ending wooden tables. Fresh fruit and cabbage were also among the food giving it small patches of colour and life amongst the decaying clutter. Hunchbacks of different sizes and shapes sat eating, chatting and playing drinking games. A couple noticed Fizbar being brought in by the neck and their large pointed pink tongues rolled wetting their lips. One of them leapt from its bench and ran towards Narrow Eyes. Narrow Eyes hit him with the butt of a mace he had pulled from his back and sent the attacker flying back to his seat. He grunted and Narrow Eyes let out a guttural and throated snarl. Fizbar noticed a large hard leather single pauldron on Narrow Eye's shoulder, a muscly shoulder of a warrior. His journal was now half-hanging from his cloak pocket. Even though his neck was numb, he began to feel it tingling, burning and pricking.

'He's going purple,' said one hunchback.

'Like an aubergine!' shouted another.

Narrow Eyes looked at Fizbar, and then his grip slackened enabling Fizbar to finally breathe normally and even to talk. As they came to a halt, Narrow Eyes released his grip altogether and Fizbar fell hard on the floor, but this time face first. *More time on the floor* he thought, but was glad just the same. The journal fell in front of him but his reflexes allowed him to quickly grab it and press it tightly to his chest, as if guarding a treasure. He panted like a dog and felt a little dizzy. He was about to ask for his wand when Plum Eyes gave it to another hunchback who sat at the foot of a long wooden table nearest to the wizard. Plum Eyes whispered in his ear and slammed the spoon down in front of him. The room fell silent. The hunchback's eyes fixed on the spoon, then darted to the wizard, and then back to the spoon once more. After a long pause he finally gestured to Plum and Narrow Eyes with a grunt whilst peering at the book Fizbar had clutched firmly to his chest. They turned and left to join the rest of their clan on the tables. The noise returned to a normal chatter and then to a more festive level.

The hunchback gestured to Fizbar to take a seat next to him on the bench. Fizbar scrutinised every characteristic. The hunchback was large, not as big as Narrow Eyes, but he had a more muscle-sculptured physique. He was dressed in clothes that looked like tailored potato sacks that were full of soil and filth. A couple of dark square patches had been badly sewn onto his sleeves, but it was enough to notice he was different and of importance. He had little hair on his head, which was normal for his race. His eyes were small and black, and folds of skin provided the sunken sockets they sat in. His eyebrows were bordering on white and they complemented his saggy black eye-bags. His nose was blunt, but long and joined his forehead, which was pronounced. His ears were like pear tomatoes and his mouth was large with the top lip falling over the lower. There was no doubt that tooth decay and thick saliva were the hallmark of his race. His hunch was big, but the deformity appeared with a measure of subtlety. He took his time, finishing a piece of deer flesh he had torn from the small cooked buck that lay on the table. He washed it down with a large cup of bubbling broth and wiped the froth from a white beard that would have looked better on his head. He burped fiercely. Fizbar's head rose, not at the sound, but the revolting smell that wafted his way. Fizbar waved a hand in front of his nose and scanned the hall. He couldn't see any exits. There was a way in; the way he had come. That was the only way out.

'You can't get out unless we let you, Wizard,' said the hunchback in a surprising voice. It was softer than Fizbar had expected, and he spoke with a subtle lisp, but his speech was much clearer than the others.

'I wasn't going anywhere.' Fizbar looked at him tearing the flesh from the cooked body. He looked at his wand on the table next to the hunchback's plate.

'Don't worry about your spoon. It's in the right place.' The hunchback laughed and then coughed as a bit of meat tickled his throat, making him spit it out and sending it flying. He swallowed hard and washed down the remaining bits of meat with a little broth. 'I am Nimvar, chief of the hunchback's and of this grove.' The hunchback gestured with outspread arms at his clan. 'What do you think?'

'You have a nice place here, except for those brutes who mishandled me.'

Nimvar gestured towards the hunchbacks. 'If it wasn't for my boys,' he pointed at Plum and Narrow, 'you wouldn't have got this far!'

Fizbar caressed his neck. 'I never knew this was here.'

'By "this" I imagine you mean the grove?'

'Yes.' Fizbar sat next to the hunchback who thought the wizard must be either very brave or stupid. 'I never knew this existed. I never even knew about so many hunchbacks, I thought…'

'That we were all dead?'

'No. Not that, I just thought you were… Scattered.'

'Scattered we are, but there are various groves across the land. Not many know of this one except for the Order of Light.' He stared at Fizbar noticing his discomfort. 'You're obviously not of the Order, so who told you?'

Fizbar now felt pressured. Still clinging to the journal, he added. 'The Lex know I have something.' He looked down at the journal reaffirming his grip. 'Gildor said you would help me understand.'

'Ahhh, Gildor. Yes… I like him. He's a funny little thing. Strange and funny to look at; noble, but unfortunately not blue-blooded,' he said through a controlled belch, his lisp vanishing for a moment. 'For a wizard you are rather unusual. You dress like a tenderfoot, and act like a frightened puppy. You aren't in the Order, are you? Unless they have lowered their standards. Has one of them died?'

'No, to both questions.' He smiled feebly. 'And to be

honest, I'm not sure why I'm here.'

'Wizards, honest? That would be a first.'

'I'm not like other wizards. I remember saying the exact same thing not so long ago to a hunchback in one of the caves of Fintar forest. He was a twin. Maybe you know him?'

Nimvar banged the table with both large fists, exposing his hairless and sculptured forearms. He blurted out, 'Meedril and Weedril!'

'You know of them?'

'Know of them! I should do, they're my sons.'

'How do you know they're your sons? They could be anyone's.' He looked around at the other hunchbacks.

'I'm the only hunchback to have ever had twins in our history. Do they both speak funny?'

'Well, the one I met did. He spoke in a an odd accent.'

'There you go then.' Nimvar paused for a second. 'He speaks like his mother. Bless her cotton threads.' He chuckled, picked a large potato and swallowed it whole. Fizbar was stunned at the ease with which he did this. He touched his throat again wincing at the soreness. The hunchback's head seemed to rest on his shoulders, and he wondered if Nimvar really did have a neck.

'The Council gave me a job as part of my advancement in wizarding ranks. I helped one of them with some nasty Korrigans, because he wasn't happy with his hump.' He stopped, thinking he might have passed the boundaries of acceptable discussion. Especially, as humps were a touchy subject amongst their race.

Nimvar nodded and humbly lowered his head like a child who had just been told off. Shame was visible and he tapped his fingers on the table in thought. 'Well… That's another story and not for your ears.' He raised his head to look straight at Fizbar, blinking his little eyes. 'You must be here for a reason. If Gildor sent you then I think I know why.'

'Did Gildor know my mother Feena Trundle? He seemed to also know my father Jack Trundle. It's confusing. I didn't get much time to ask as the Lex Talionis appeared out of the blue.' Fizbar touched the base of his neck gingerly.

'They have a habit of doing that,' replied Nimvar. 'But they can't get in here. Stupid if they try.'

'That's reassuring.'

'I don't know how much I can help, but I'll try.'

Fizbar nodded. 'I just don't know why all of this has surfaced now. Even why I was given this journal – a stupid blank journal.' He loosened his grip on the book. Watchfully, he laid it on the table, next to the spoon.

'Your wand is quiet,' said Nimvar.

'He doesn't speak much when others are around. Unless he trusts them.'

'A wise wand.' Nimvar smiled, cleared his throat and sat quietly. He held his lips together as he thought. The oil from the meat shone on his lips as the light hit them. 'There is a lot you truly don't know. What does the great and almighty Overlord have to say? Has he told you anything?'

'No. He's been pretty defensive, unwilling to talk about it. He's strange; wears the Zalbar burden on his sleeve.'

'Hmmm,' replied Nimvar. He accepted Fizbar's sincerity and made strange sounds, like forcing air through tight lips before wiping them with a dirty rag.

'All right.' He got up and shouted to the hunchbacks in the hall to leave them. Many were reluctant, grumpy and some even carried on eating. Nimvar threw some chicken bones at Plum and Narrow eyes, gesturing for them to take charge of the matter. With some pushing and pulling the two hunchbacks soon had the room clear; with the last two being thrown out through the entrance. Fizbar was again impressed by their strength. It appeared that not many hunchbacks were prepared to argue with them. Finally the hall was silent but the smell was as strong as ever.

Narrow Eyes was the last to leave, his head lowered to the chief as he departed. Nimvar lifted himself from his seat and cracked his back. His hump wasn't as significant as the others, especially Plum Eyes whose hump was twice the size of Nimvar's. His gait was more human-like as he crossed his arms and paced around. It seemed hard for him to speak and he made several attempts to. Finally he spoke.

'Our kind has been forced to live like this,' he gestured to his surroundings, 'since the revolt. Almost twenty years ago, give or take a few.'

'I know about the revolt,' said Fizbar.

'No you don't!' He pointed at the wizard in anger. 'Most of you know only what you are taught. It's a big subject in your schools. The history of Sintar in all its falsity! But a history nonetheless, with many well kept secrets and weasely oaths.'

'Falsity?' Fizbar looked at his wand.

Nimvar turned; his back to the wizard. 'Yes. Hunchbacks and wizards were harmonious. They've been together since time began, or thereabouts; thinking that nothing could ever come between them, but long ago it all changed. Something did come between them. Some wizards entered a forest with a book. A powerful book, one that—'

'The Grimoire!' He cut the hunchback short.

'This is not a guessing game. Who's telling this? You or me?' said the hunchback, resting his hands on his waist.

'You are. Sorry.'

Nimvar recomposed himself and paced freely again. 'Wizards back then had a different scheme of their own. They wanted to bind the powers of The Grimoire. Merge magic to their physical form, therefore relinquishing the need of a wand.'

Fizbar looked at the journal and automatically realised its importance and worried about its owner. 'But that isn't possible. Binding magic isn't possible. It's pure and you can't mess purity.' There was no expression that Fizbar could read on Nimvar's face. 'Can you?' he asked.

Nimvar stretched his fingers and crunched his knuckles, which made Fizbar flinch at the sound. 'They teach you that in school. A hoodwinking idea. They feed you falsities like fish in a fish tank, keeping your inquisitive minds away from tampering with possibilities affecting the magical graces.' He paused. 'Geldahar Zalbar was an inquisitive mind that would not only defy the Overlord and other wizards, but the laws of magic in their entirety. He researched well and spent years whilst at school collecting the information he needed to cast the biggest spell this world would ever witness. If he had succeeded, the world would have been an evil place.'

'I think he did succeed. With the Lex Talionis I don't see it getting any better.'

Nimvar raised his voice slightly. 'My boy! If Zalbar had succeeded, you wouldn't be here talking to me right now.' His eyes opened wide, this time like saucers. He felt he had let out a little too much information.

Fizbar listened attentively. 'What do you mean by that?' His arm was on the journal as he followed Nimvar's stride. The hunchback loved a good story telling.

'Your mother Feena was a believer in the old ways of

magic, before wizardry was accepted as the safest path. Sacrifice was the way of obtaining magical graces, if you were gifted that is.'

'What changed?'

'Wands as the channel for magic became a kind of contract, in order to use and control magic. That meant sacrifice was practiced less, until it became obsolete.'

'So the old methods were useless?' He was interested.

'Some believed so.'

'How so?'

'They caused more grief, pain and suffering than anything else. The suffering left behind was deemed evil so this path quickly died out. Until your mother brought it back.'

He thought back a step. 'You said sacrifice. What's my mother got to do with that?'

'Sacrificing a wizard meant that the magical plane could be accessed. Open to all kinds of possibilities and experiments. Your mother stole The Grimoire, before a magical lock was cast on it. She tried to perform a sacrifice in hope of accessing the plane so she could bind her magic to her life force. If she had succeeded then wands would have ceased to exist.'

'But... But... Therolius told me the first person to steal The Grimoire was Gelorg.' He was confused by all this information. 'It was just a test... Wasn't it?' He scratched his head.

The hunchback laughed. 'I'm afraid that was what you would call a white lie.'

'What would you call it then?'

'A lie,' said Nimvar, 'one told to protect. Zalbar dug deeper to unearth the truth.'

'And how would you know all of this then.'

'I have my reasons.'

'And what are they?'

'Mine alone.'

Fizbar twiddled his fingers whilst staring at his wand. 'So my mother tried to perform a sacrifice?' he asked, not really wanting to know the answer.

'Yes, she tried.'

'What did she use? A goat, sheep?' He thought for some other small animals. 'A deer, fox, rabbit – a pheasant? A goose, but please don't say a wizard—'

'A baby,' Nimvar cut in.

'Baby!' said Fizbar in shock. He trembled slightly, and a draft forced him to wrap up warm.

'I'm afraid that's not all.'

'What could be worse than that? My mother used a baby in hope of performing some stupid offering to magic.'

'The baby was rescued by Gildor, and Therolius.'

'Gildor and Therolius were with my mother?' He was again surprised.

'Yes, but not the way you're thinking.'

'They stopped her?'

'In a way, yes.'

'They saved the baby?'

'Yes.'

'Who was the baby?' asked Fizbar, his voice a little rocky and dry.

Nimvar avoided a direct answer. 'She was ill. Numerous people had fed lies to her. Wizards fell at her feet and she felt she possessed supreme power. Her lust was focused on the ultimate prize. Sacrifice a part of her to receive the greatest gift of all. She felt this would be better than a normal sacrifice. So she offered you to the old ways. She thought that by sacrificing you, she would bind magic and rule the world.'

'Sorry?' Fizbar's face was blank and pale. 'I thought for a moment there you said *me*.'

Nimvar finally sat down and rested his chin on his knuckles, releasing a deep sigh. 'That's what I said.'

The news was coming too quickly and Fizbar didn't know how to take it all in. *It's a lie*, he thought, *the hunchback's lying*. He looked at Nimvar, *but why would he lie?* His wand was silent so he couldn't ask him for any help or explanation. He thought that if his wand had known anything about this it would have told him. He didn't know what to say or think. He was in a muddle.

'But I was her son. This can't be true.' Fizbar cupped his head in his hands, his elbows extended on the table mirroring Nimvar.

'I am not here to reason with you, Fizbar, or make excuses for her actions. I'm doing as the Order of Light requested. Telling you the truth. Would you like me to stop?'

'The Order of Light... Doing as they requested?'

'Yes, Gildor and the rest of the wizards. The Order was created essentially to protect The Grimoire.'

'Great! I suppose next you're going to tell me I play a part in all this,' he said.

'Oh yes.' Nimvar's large hand touched Fizbar, '... I've hardly begun yet!'

14

The Fourth Journal

'I'll be back later Helena.'

'I'd prefer it if you called me Mother.'

Hetty smiled and said in a teasing tone, 'Mother.'

'That's better.' She glanced at her wand. It uncoiled from her hand as she placed it by a jar on the table. 'Where are you going anyway? I thought you were going to help me with the inventory? Especially after Fizbar's sabotage.'

'Don't you mean epic entrance?'

'That's what I said. I need it all spick and span for the first day of trade.'

'I'll finish it off later for you. I need to collect some ingredients for one of those broken jars,' said Hetty whilst pointing at a jar that sat next to a swamp plant. It read, "Franshires from Frangar's swamp".

Helena's head shot up at once. 'I don't want you going there, it's dangerous! Many wizards have used the swamp grounds for testing their stupid hovering and reappearing spells, as well as others.' She sighed deeply and placed both hands on her hips. 'That spot is famous for those long distance journeys; failed ones I might add. You know where it gets its name from don't you?'

'Yes,' replied Hetty, slumping her shoulders in expectation of yet another storytelling.

'It was named after the last wizard to die there attempting one of those hovering landings. Other more experienced and capable wizards have—'

'I know mother. They've never made the attempt. Don't worry; I'll be fine, I just need some Franshires, which grow a good few feet from the swamp's famous spot. I'll be safe. Besides, one I'm not a wizard, and two I use conventional transport.'

'That's doesn't make me feel any better,' said Helena with an air of concern. She walked up to her daughter and, in a motherly way brushed the shoulders of her jacket. 'You and your inquisitive mind can both be led astray.' She glanced at the giant swamp plants as they swayed at the mention of the "swamp".

Hetty brushed her hair aside, put a clip in her mouth and attempted a ponytail. 'I'll be fine. Stop worrying,' she said through the clip in her mouth.

'Worrying is a mother's job. It's also something I've been doing for a long time before you were born.'

Hetty pulled and straightening her tweed jacket, then opened the door. The bell rang.

'And another thing, Hetty.' Helena called out, stretching

her neck.

Hetty glanced back through the door at her mother, waiting for the final speech.

'Stay away from that Fizbar. He'll only get you into trouble.'

Hetty didn't say anything, but managed a half convincing smile as she left, closing the door and leaving the ringing behind her.

Helena stared momentarily at her wand and said, 'Things are going to get considerably worse from now on.' Her wand didn't reply, and she didn't expect it to. She picked up a pen; then carried on with her inventory, dipping her head further into the parchment. The bell rang again. 'What have you forgotten now?' she asked idly as she put the pen down and picked up a jar examining the label and squinting her eyes at the fine print. Large rounded glasses sat on the end of her nose as she focused hard on the small print. There was no reply, so she glanced over one corner of the parchment. The jar fell to the table and the lid popped open and rolled until it hit the floor. Her body became rigid. Her hand reached for her wand, but it was no use. It flew to the far side of the shop; next to a tall book-shelving unit. The lid still spun on the floor.

'Tut-tut-tut! I'm not so easily thwarted, Helena.'

Viktor Witfar walked towards her. Denrick and Dinfar followed close by, as if stuck together with glue. A faun closed the door and the bell rang again. It guarded the door from the outside, like a bouncer. Denrick pointed a pair of scissors at the spinning lid and a bolt of electricity erupted from its end and the lid vanished.

'There, that's better,' he said in a rough, grating voice.

Denrick's arms were muscly and his forearms were wide; his left was covered with red, leafy tattoos that crawled up his shoulder and neck to the lobe of his ear. His black shirt was fitted tightly and was sleeveless and his black trousers stuck to his legs like tights. His face was pale and a pointy chin matched his nose in length. His eyes looked small, black and empty; but it was his spiky blue punk-like hair that was the most striking feature.

Helena looked at Dinfar who differed from his twin, only in having a higher pitched voice and spiky green punk-like hair. He stood with an outstretched arm and pointed his wand, a bottle of hair gel at Helena in a threatening manner.

'What do you want?' said Helena with a tremor in her voice, 'And why have you brought the Hex brothers with you? Can't do anything on your own?' She felt defenceless without her wand.

'I think you know what we are here for,' said Denrick.

Helena looked blank and pursed her lips.

Viktor glared back at Denrick. 'Thank you, but I'll do the talking from now on.' He turned to fix his good eye on Helena. 'I'll give you two clues. One, it's a book, and two, it contains *your* spells.' He paced left and right. Viktor's description was quite sufficient for Helena to know what he was after, but she chose not to respond. 'It's a journal. *Your journal*.' He pointed at her two times.

'Yeah! Hand it over flower woman!' Denrick spouted out with a supportive glance from his brother.

'Intimidation has never been your strong point has it, Denrick,' said Viktor, not expecting an answer.

Dinfar sniggered at his brother.

'I wouldn't laugh if I were you, Dinfar.'

The sniggering stopped.

'Why do you want my journal anyway?' asked Helena.

'Ah! Well…' Viktor withdrew his feather and pointed it at Helena in a threatening manner, reinforcing his dominance in the room. 'A little birdie told us that your journal was here, somewhere hidden in this shop to be precise.' He scanned the room.

'Who is this person?' said Helena with concern, 'And what could they possibly know about my journal? I destroyed it, just like the Overlord instructed all those years ago.' She knew who had revealed the location. It had to be her shop assistant, Medra. She was the only one who knew and Zalbar must have forced the information out of her. She felt sick at the thought of Medra in Zalbar's hands. 'The Overlord…'

Viktor burst into laughter. The twins looked at each other, and then joined in, not because they understood the joke, but because they felt it might placate Viktor.

'The Overlord,' said Viktor. The atmosphere in the room was now tenser than ever. His un-patched eye started to twitch as the pitch of his voice rose. 'You needn't worry about him.' He withdrew a note from an inside pocket and waved it at Helena. 'We all know about your affection for him and your secret pitiful love for Jack Trundle. That's why your journal is so important. It's part of my master's grand plan.' He lowered the note. 'In fact the Overlord will be here very soon.' Viktor pointed his feather at the piece of paper and the note disappeared, like glitter in the wind. 'He should be receiving this note even as we speak.'

'What note?' said Helena.

'The one that will say Zalbar has kidnapped you and if he wants you alive he must turn up at the altar.'

Helena didn't reply. She looked half in shock, as though she had been expecting this.

'Zalbar has a plan for the wondrous Therolius,' Viktor added.

'Therolius represents the good in us all and he'll…'

Viktor's snigger grew into laughter again, so much so that he bent forward to rest his hands on his knees. His stomach ached from laughter. 'Good! Ha ha!' He composed himself and sniffed. 'He's the reason for all of this mess and for your information Zalbar is the real victim.'

'Zalbar is no victim. He is pure vileness,' she said in disgust, and feeling the need to protect the Overlord's goodness. 'Therolius should have silenced him forever all those years ago. The burden he carries is unjust. He should have finished him back at the school. That would have been worthy cause for a burden.'

Viktor paced; his hands behind his back, twiddling his feather and crunching his nose like a rabbit. The twins had their wands fixed, at the ready, and aimed at Helena. 'Well, you'll soon see the light. So will he in fact, but first I have orders to bring you both to our lord. You and your journal.'

'He may be your lord but he's no lord of mine. You're all outcasts, even the people of Sintar and Fintar think of you as the vile. And how dare you barge in here and…'

'Hold that sour tongue! For once just shut it!' Viktor raised his feather; his face red and full of agitation and his form flickered a few times in anger. Helena smiled at his wand. He noticed it and his eyes followed hers. 'Let's see what you think about these wands now then.' He thrust his feather at her and spoke, 'Boys!'

The brothers sneered and jumped up immediately and started to ransack the place. Pulling jars maliciously off the shelves and discharging bolts of light at various spots. Containers crashed on the floor; some crashed in the air. Powders mixed together, and puffs of smoke ensued. Plants were pulled from their roots and you could hear their low drones and cries. Dinfar wrestled with a giant swamp plant and found it difficult to aim his wand at it so his brother helped and cast a spell, which made them all flop. An electricity bolt jumped from one plant to another like a virus and they all fell heavily to the floor. A smell similar to burnt flesh circled the shop and the plants rattled.

The faun peered through the glass door and raised its upper lip exposing its teeth, laughing frantically; stamping on the ground like a spoilt child. An old couple approached the shop and the faun roared at them. They immediately turned and ran in fear. It then returned its attention to the commotion inside, laughing; its pink tongue dangling and the warm moist breath steamed the window.

Viktor's smile grew as Helena's hands shot to her face, cupping her grief and cries of despair. She shared the pain and anguish of her plants. Her shop was being ruined right before her eyes, and she could do nothing.

'You can stop this! Just give me what I want.' Viktor's arm was still pointing at her more purposefully than ever. Her hand slowly dripped down her right cheek, until she finally pointed to a black jar that sat alone on a shelf.

'In there?' Viktor asked with an inquisitive eye.

She nodded reluctantly, and then wiped a falling tear. Dinfar used his wand and zapped a set of collapsible stairs. Denrick walked up them. He lifted himself up the last three steps and grabbed the jar that sat alone, high on the shelf. It was dusty. Dinfar coughed. He rested it between his chest and the shelves; it was bulky and awkward to open. He prized it open just like a little a child would a jar of sweets. His face gleamed at the content inside and he lifted it up and nodded to Viktor.

'There, that wasn't so difficult was it?'

'You won't know how to use it or read it. Only I know how.'

'You're right,' Viktor replied. 'I don't know, but Zalbar does.'

After thumping down the stairs Dinfar handed the journal to Viktor who blew a little dust from the cover and opened it. He looked through it without focus on the contents. He only wanted to show Helena she had failed to keep it safe and to gloat.

'The pages smell lovely.' He shut the journal and popped it into a pocket, close to his chest. 'Take her.' Viktor gestured towards the door.

The Hex brothers grabbed her by the wrists.

'How dare you! Take your hands off me. You're hurting me.' She struggled, but to no avail. The brothers were too strong and her attempts to wriggle free were in vain.

Victor leant on the counter, picked up a pen and started scribbling on a piece of parchment. He then tore it. 'Load her up!' he shouted.

As they dragged her out, Helena dropped a gold medallion on the floor by the counter. Viktor and the twins didn't notice it. The Hex brothers opened the door and the bell rang. The faun threw back a large black canvas that was draped over the back of a black wagon. Then the twins threw her into the empty wagon and the faun jumped in with her; fastening the canvas door shut behind him. The twins leapt into the wagon and then left the street.

'Zalbar's waiting, Overlord.' Victor smiled, 'And for you Fizbar, enjoy the note.' He then puffed into black strands of liquid-smoke. The door of the shop flew wide open, the bell not ringing this time.

15

The Magic Duel

The Overlord ran as fast as a man of his age could, grasping the note. He thought about using magic to transport him there in hope of ending this once and for all, but something in him advised against using magic while in a heated temper. His cloak caught the bottom of his shoes as he ran, and for the fourth time he nearly lost his footing. He was anxious, angry and at the same time full of remorse. He waved away branches that blocked his path, barely noticing the ones that scratched his face. The peaty and muddy ground was damp with mixed leaf and other broken-down vegetation that squished with every footstep. He was sweating profusely and it had been a long while since he had had to exert himself like this. Under the forest canopy and across the ground he ran as though he were roller-skating. The colour of the tree trunks turned from brown to black as he made his way deeper into the forest. The air was cold and night was arriving. Reaching a clearing, he knew he was there and he knew who was waiting for him, but he was prepared. Therolius slowed to a walking pace. Red faced and breathing heavily, he coughed a few times and winced at the pain from his dry throat. Finally he could make out the appearance of the altar in the distance. As he moved closer, wand at the ready, he could see Helena on the sacrificial altar; motionless. He hurried to her and cupped her head with his hands. She didn't react. He checked to see if she was breathing and was relieved when he saw her chest rise and fall. As he recomposed himself he panned around, feeling alone in the large clearing, but quickly realising that he wasn't. The trees a hundred yards from the altar swayed in the same cold wind that touched his scratched face. A figured appeared a few feet from the Overlord. It was Zalbar.

'Therolius Delrunt, how good to meet you again.' Zalbar hovered closer to the Overlord, almost effortlessly, his face just inches from the Therolius's. Therolius already had his wand fixed on Zalbar who mimicked his spell-casting pose. Each anticipated the other's move.

'Do you really think your wand is up to it? Attacking me a second time won't solve anything.' Therolius could only stare at Zalbar; and his adrenaline levels began to soar.

Zalbar took his time before replying. 'Two wizards, out alone… At dusk… In the woods. Almost creepy wouldn't you say?'

Therolius noticed that Zalbar didn't actually grip his wand and that it was bound to his forearm with vines. 'One wizard you mean,' he said wetting his dry lips before continuing in a harsh and commanding voice. He didn't take his eyes off Zalbar's wand. 'I told you all those years ago, you're no wizard. Wizards don't go against the grace. You're still that empty little boy I pulled out of the orphanage. I should have ended it whilst I had the chance the day you tried to steal The Grimoire.'

Therolius glanced at Helena who lay still on the altar. 'Let her go, she has nothing to do with this,' he said.

'I can't do that. I'm sorry, Overlord, but she has everything to do with it! You really should have silenced me back then. But I was young and careless and your focus on the best in everybody ignores their other sides. I can assure you that I won't be as careless as then. You see, I have learnt so much since our last... Encounter, thanks to Gimera.'

'Gimera? What's the Archmage got to do with this?' said Therolius.

Zalbar sighed deeply. 'You're supposed to know everything, but clearly you don't. It was Gimera who pulled me out from that stinking orphanage and if it wasn't for him I'd be disgraced, full of self-pity and consumed by guilt.' He glanced at the Overlord who now felt threatened. Zalbar's face, or rather the void of mist in its place, looked cold, dark and empty, but Therolius could read it, he could sense the same apprehension and anxiety as he did all those years ago.

'Guilt? Why would you feel guilt?' asked Therolius.

'Me? I don't feel guilt. I know who my parents were and they too were cursed by society. I've always known who I was from the very beginning and it was all thanks to you. It's you who carries the guilt and disappointment; the shame.' He paced. 'It was Gimera who assured me you'd pay me a visit; enrol me for the tenderfoots.'

'What are you implying? Are you trying to pin your unfortunate actions and feelings upon Gimera and me? Your parents were ill; the magic they possessed was too powerful for their abilities. Channelling your anger would…'

'I would never do that, Therolius. I am here to thank you for putting everything into perspective for me, as one would say.'

'I didn't need Gimera to show me your potential, but why the anger and lust for power? It's not too late—'

'Don't presume to think you know what's best for me old man!' Zalbar shouted in anger. 'Don't patronise me, Therolius! I never converted to these ways. I was destined to rule.' He gave himself the once over with open arms. 'Apart from the face I think I seem very fitting.'

Zalbar floated across the ground, his cloak flapping with the breeze, and away from the sacrificial altar.

Therolius tightened his grip on his wand who, as

always, had nothing to say. Knowing he wouldn't get any response, he whispered to his wand anyway. 'If there was ever a time I needed you, it is now my friend.'

'Ever since you took me under your wing…'

'I never took you under my wing! I treated all my students with the same integrity and oversight that any Overlord should.'

'Oh! I apologise, I didn't mean it that way Therolius. You opened me up to a world I was fit for, with a little help from others along the way. The world of magic was there to be understood and then used by someone with the courage to grasp it.' He emphasised this by closing his skeletal grasp tightly around his staff, pointing it directly at the wizard.

'You are mad. Completely! Nobody can ever understand fully the origins of magic let alone seek to control it. I told you that back then, and nothing has changed.'

Zalbar tutted. 'Oh but it has, and that's where you are wrong.'

'Then please enlighten me.'

'Here's what I'll do. I'll tell you what you want to know. Then you'll hand over your wand and then—'

'You'll kill me?' Therolius finished the sentence with a question. 'How original and considerate.'

Zalbar caressed his imaginary chin in a sneaky manner. 'That's one possibility; but unfortunately I still have a use for you. However, after that I will end your reign by taking your place.'

Therolius looked at Zalbar's empty face and pursed his lips together, pondering. Then he chuckled. 'That's absurd! You'll never take my place.'

Zalbar let out an amplified laugh that even startled the birds as they fled the treetops. 'I'll give you a chance. How about a duel?'

Therolius narrowed his brow. 'The old fashioned way?'

'Just like you Overlord, old fashioned.'

'You're giving me an option?'

'Not really, just trying to be polite after all the years between us. It'll give you time to reconsider your position.' Zalbar stared at the wizard, his body waiting and still; the only part of him moving was his void of a face.

After a moment Therolius spoke. 'Very well. But I assure you it will be unpleasant.'

'I wouldn't expect it any other way.'

'Just get on with it and shut that mouth, wherever it used to be.'

'MEEDRIL!' shouted Zalbar.

The hunchback appeared.

'Meedril?' Therolius felt it hard to say his name.

'Yes, Master.'

Meedril shuffled over to the altar, and glanced at Helena bypassing the Overlord's questioning face.

'Keep an eye on this wench. The Overlord and I have business to settle.'

The hunchback moved closer.

'Oh, and finish the preparations.'

'What preparations?' asked Therolius, but his question was ignored.

They both took their positions. Then the two wizards turned back to back.

'Remember, wands out, fully stretched arms and the turn at the count of twenty paces.' Zalbar ordered.

'You don't have to lecture me on the rules of conduct.'

'Sometimes I forget who the teacher is,' he laughed.

Upon reaching the twenty paces they whizzed around. Therolius had his wand outstretched, at full arm's length. Zalbar had his staff tilted as it was now in the same hand that had the wand strapped to it. Therolius conjured first.

'*Arboreus Silvanus!*' he shouted and a green light shot from the tip of his wand and into the trees, which began to sway; then the leaves rustled vigorously, and the wind blew violently. A dull thumping sound grew in volume as it approached and suddenly a large tree troll burst from the tree line. Its long arms and legs looked like sculptured tree trunks in human form. The bucket-like mouth and human-styled nose sat on a spiky and wild-branched face. It was completely brown with moss and lichen gracing its contours. Its elbows spiked out like wild forks and its back was full of wild spiralling and free moving wooded coils covered by creeping plants. Its abdomen was slender and a lichen patch filled what was the groin. Its piercing blue eyes looked down at the wizard and loud stomps crashed the ground as it walked and stood in front of him in a threatening pose. It was a remarkable beast and a true spirit of what the forest elements stood for.

'Ah!' said Zalbar, 'I see we're going floral, *Kelpius evoco!*' he shouted in the same loud, menacing tone and a yellow light glowed from the wand, spread along his staff and shot from the end of it. Therolius was shocked at Zalbar using a staff. He was confused. Staffs were only a symbol of higher wizardry, a decoration. They weren't used as wands. It was then that Therolius began to worry for Sintar's safety, as well as his own.

The wind blew again menacingly and the ground started to rumble behind the evil wizard. The earth started to crack open, rock and mounds of earth tumbled over each other as a giant floral headdress emerged from the ground. The earth trembled more and a leafy plant-like structure shot out of the ground. A small array of purple and cerulean blue flowers sat in the middle of a bush of broad shiny oval leaves. The headdress was followed by a large root-like creature with a straggly root-beard and a row of razor-like teeth. It screamed and clenched its teeth before making a chomping sound. It emitted a high ear-piercing scream that even made the troll's head tilt a little. It was a mandragora, a demon of the soil. The roots crawled across the ground as it shuffled along in search of prey, stopping in front of Zalbar.

'I know Fizbar has the journal!' Zalbar shouted.

'And why would you say that?' the Overlord shot back.

'Because Gimera told me he has it. Besides, Fizbar also opened the book.'

Therolius realised his mistake. Gimera had been working against him.

'I'm surprised you didn't know. Even Gildor suspected a traitor in the Order. He knew Gimera wouldn't stay true to you for very long.'

Therolius felt anger and shouted instructing the troll to advance. As the troll thumped on the ground towards him, Zalbar reacted and the mandragora shuffled forward. Both giants walked closer to each other until contact was made and the fight began. The troll lifted its arms and began to twirl quickly. The mandragora's roots crawled to the troll's feet and pulled hard at them. The troll fell heavy to the ground, but as it did its large wooden hands clipped the headdress of the mandragora, ripping off some of the broad leaves and purple flowers. A scream filled the air and the roots retracted immediately however they had already wrapped around the troll's legs and in retracting pulled hard, crashing the troll to the ground. It blinked its blue eyes at Therolius who leapt back shocked as the troll nearly flattened him. The wizard's rule was that none of them could move. The troll looked back at the mandragora, which started to scream; shaking its headdress. The roots advanced again as the troll lifted himself up, grabbing them before they could inflict any damage. The troll pulled hard, wrapping the roots around his arm like a spindle, and the mandragora was hauled closer and closer. The tug of war intensified as the mandragora resisted spitting out roots from behind to anchor itself and to pull towards safety. Other roots crept their way up the tree troll, but it brushed them off like dried spaghetti with its free hand. The mandragora finally gave way and was pulled close to the troll who released the roots only to grab the mandragora's vulnerable neck. The mandragora bit the troll's arm with its sharp teeth, causing the troll to let out a dull drone that resembled a foghorn. The sound startled the mandragora and a root whipped past Zalbar. He ducked. Therolius smiled only briefly as Zalbar managed to maintain his position. The mandragora then whipped its roots around the troll and grabbed its beard. The troll became incapacitated and let out another earthy drone. The mandragora had the upper hand. The troll could not release his arms, but it turned and with its large feet thrust forward at the trunk of the mandragora. The troll broke free and with a last wave of energy lunged at the mandragora pushing it back to where it had originally risen. As it crashed on the ground branches flew into the air and leaves scattered the ground. The mandragora lay motionless as the troll moved towards it. The mandragora's roots were torn, but in vain they still attempted to lash out at the tree-troll's face. He brushed them away and began to tear at the rooted giant with both hands and an occasional stomp of the foot. The troll let out another drone and then the tearing became less violent as the plant lay motionless. The troll looked at Therolius with its piercing blue eyes, and with what seemed to be a smile it too slowly made its way back towards where it had come from. Therolius looked around for Zalbar, but he was nowhere to be seen. Seconds passed and Therolius took the opportunity to approach Meedril who was lurched over Helena. Suddenly he felt as if he were paralysed. He had only felt like this once in his life and that was a long time ago and in Zalbar's presence. The Overlord's eyes moved frantically trying to locate the source of his constriction, but he already knew what had happened.

'Not so fast!' A voice came from the mandragora as Zalbar emerged from behind the large motionless headdress. 'That's twice you've let your guard down. But this time there is no evading the spell. I'm afraid, old man that you'll stay like this until I die. This is unlikely ever to happen.'

He drifted over to the altar as the dead plant began to wither away. As he did it slowly fell, sliding back into the hole in the earth and the soil began to cover it over. He whispered in the Overlord's ear. 'Gypsy magic! That's old school. Thought you were immune to it.' He laughed. 'Now with just another piece of the puzzle to finish, I assure you it will finish pretty soon.'

'What should I do?' asked Meedril in keeping with his lack of acumen.

'Wait for my instructions,' said Zalbar, dipping his skeletal hand into Therolius's pocket and pulling out his journal. 'I knew you always carried your journal with you. I even know you used to carry mine. But thanks to Gimera it won't be difficult to get it from a Falzard.'

Zalbar placed the journal on the sacrificial altar. 'I mean, why him? I can't believe you put all your eggs in one empty basket. Why choose a Falzard?' He pulled out another journal that belonged to Helena and placed it next to Therolius's on the stone altar. 'Look at that. Family reunited. Well, for the time being.' He pointed his wand arm at Helena. '*Evigilo aliquammultus!*'

Suddenly her eyes popped open, but she could not speak or move.

'There now. Look at you both. You know the spell. Sad thing is you can't use it.'

Therolius's eyes were fixed on Zalbar's wrist. Zalbar noticed his questioning eyes and turned it over.

'Yes, lovely isn't it? I don't need my hand on the wand. As long as it is touching my physical form it's enough, well for the time being anyway. Time has taught me many things, and you're about to see it get a lot better.'

He quickly hid his hand. 'It's nearly time.' He pressed his head next to the Overlord, and whispered. 'What? Sorry... I can't hear you. Gypsy magic did you say?' He laughed again and shouted, 'Meedril! Bring me the other journals.'

Zalbar lowered his head towards Helena and Therolius. '*I have five journals.*' he whispered. 'Feena's is on its way to me now.' Then Zalbar raised his head displaying his wand and staff. 'And with any good fortune the seventh should arrive pretty soon after that.'

16

The Truth

They both stared blankly at each other, waiting for someone to break the silence. Nimvar looked calm and relaxed, and with every move Fizbar leaned forward anticipating the hunchback's next words.

'Go on then! Begin,' said Fizbar.

The hunchback took a slow, deep breath. 'Therolius, Gimera, Helena and Gildor followed them to Fintar forest. To the ancient burial ground, near the lakes edge.'

'Helena was there?'

'Yes, there were six of them.'

'This just gets better!' Fizbar caressed his forehead for relief. 'Who were they?' he added, flicking a hand into the air gesturing for Nimvar to continue his story.

'You don't need to know them all, just the ones there on that night.'

Fizbar thought hard, his eyebrows pulled tight as he concentrated. 'I remember a… Memory, a flashback of some sort. I don't know what it is. Even my wand is confused, I think. I witnessed something, a band of hunchbacks with lit torches and—'

'You've seen the uprising, the past. The revolt.' Nimvar cut in.

'The revolt? Does this have something to do with my mother? Did she cause it?' He scrunched his face like a piece of crumpled up paper.

'Not entirely.' Nimvar gestured with his hand, like a scale tilting from one side to the other.

'What then? Why did I see the revolt? And why is it always in the same place?' asked Fizbar.

Nimvar grunted. 'I believe you were approaching the place where your mother initiated the ritual, the sacrifice. Seeing the past with present eyes, means you are magically bound to something, like the forest. More than that is beyond me. Therolius could explain more about that.' He shrugged his muscled shoulders.

'All right, but if the order knew about this, why did they let it get so far? They could have stopped her, couldn't they?' said Fizbar.

'I suppose to catch *them* in the act. They weren't sure about what would happen with or to The Grimoire. It's better to accuse someone when you've caught them red-handed.'

'Sometimes that leads to more problems.'

'It's the only way the Order could find out why they wanted The Grimoire.' Nimvar wiped his mouth; then drank a little more broth.

'Would my mother have really... Sacrificed me?' Fizbar paused for a moment, thinking about his mother and the disappointment this new realization entailed. He still couldn't entirely believe what Nimvar was saying.

Nimvar avoided a direct answer. 'She was not well in the head, Fizbar. Therolius felt she had completely lost her way. He knew she'd taken The Grimoire.'

'Hang on a minute, you said they.' Fizbar cut in.

'Huh?'

'Just a moment ago you said "to catch them in the act," who is them?'

Nimvar cleared his throat with a raspy cough then swallowed deeply jerking his neck as he did. 'The order had been monitoring both Rufus and Feena for a while. They let them take you and The Grimoire, but things didn't go... According to plan.'

'You've already said she wasn't well. You haven't answered my question.' Fizbar was firm.

'Given the chance, I believe she would have, yes. But the Order wouldn't have allowed it to get that far.'

'From what you're telling me, she got close enough!'

'Therolius arrived with Mersden, Zalbar's grandfather, just in time. Gildor and Gimera were there and managed to contain Feena for a while. She was wild, livid and also very clever in using her magic. It was a volatile situation.'

'You know a lot about this. If I didn't know any better I

would say that you were there,' said Fizbar.

When Nimvar didn't reply he knew there was more to it. Nimvar wiped his nose again, this time trailing his nose up his arm, sniffing a couple of times as he did.

'You *were* there,' Fizbar pressed, closely examining the hunchback's reaction. He felt he already knew the answer.

Nimvar nodded. 'I was there. Most of the hunchbacks were there, except for the old ones who have now sadly passed away.'

'Most of the hunchbacks?'

'Yes, the revolt. It started that very night.'

'My mother caused the revolt? What about Rufus?'

'Whilst Therolius was trying to deal with Feena he ignored the fact that there was a bigger problem. Jack ran out in front of Rufus.'

'You mean Jack, my father?'

'Yes, and Rufus Zalbar, Geldahar's father.'

'This just gets better. Why did my father run after Rufus?'

'It was all because of your mother. They both loved her.'

'A lover's squabble? Whilst I was on the sacrificial altar nearing my death, my father was more concerned about a lovers tiff!' Fizbar was both annoyed and disappointed.

'It was more than that, young wizard. And for the record, many men loved your mother. Many would have died for her. Even if she hadn't had the advantage of being blue-blooded.'

'I knew my mother was a blue-blood. Therolius told me a while ago. He also told me that I wasn't,' Fizbar added quickly with a hint of dejection.

'Your father went straight for Rufus, his rage fuelled by jealousy and betrayal.'

'What happened between Jack and Rufus?'

'Rufus killed him. He was too strong and your father...'

There was no reaction from Fizbar, he felt that no further surprises could either lift or lower his spirits. His wand remained very quiet, as if it too were listening carefully to the hunchback's tale.

'Therolius forced Mersden to intervene, to stop the magic duel, but he couldn't kill his son.'

'Don't tell me, Rufus killed his father.'

'How did you know? Did you see that in a vision?' asked Nimvar, wide-eyed.

'No.' Fizbar lifted his head. 'It's was just obvious something like that was going to happen. Greed and lust are powerful but predictable evils.'

Nimvar agreed and grabbed a large goblet and cleaned it with his tunic. Fizbar curled a lip with disgust. The hunchback poured some liquid into the goblet and pushed it towards the wizard. 'It's water.'

'It didn't look that colour when you poured it.'

Nimvar's forehead rumpled, the creases and folds looked funny. 'It's dark in here, and the light's deceiving, that's all.'

Fizbar pushed the goblet away. 'What else happened?'

'Therolius led the Order. A simple group of wizards formed to *oversee*, not *protect*, The Grimoire. Therolius had more of a burden than any other person, because he had caused the revolt.'

Fizbar spun the goblet around without purpose, it made a grating sound as it scraped across the wooden table. 'What happened to my mother then?' he asked. 'I was told she died giving birth to me. Obviously that was a lie.' He placed his hand firmly on the journal. Nimvar's eyes followed the wizard's actions. He could see the story was taking its toll on him.

'Your father, Jack, also followed your mother. Therolius wasn't aware of this. Jack ran out at Rufus, and it all happened far too quickly. If it's any consolation, I don't think he felt anything.'

Fizbar's eyes welled and he said, choking a little: 'You mean he died protecting my mother?' He wasn't used to being dealt so many discomforts all at once. 'I was told he ran away; left me in an alley, outside *Best Friends Forever*.'

'Maybe there is a subtle irony in that, but Jack died in a battle against Zalbar's father. He didn't stand a chance. Rufus was a truly gifted wizard; your father was only a psychic, a wizard's aid. That's what we hunchbacks were.'

'My father was a psychic?' He looked up at Nimvar.

'You didn't know?' Nimvar pointed to the goblet. 'Drink. I'm surprised you've been kept in the dark all this time.'

Reluctantly Fizbar pinched his nose and drank. He didn't want to distract the hunchback as he wanted to hear the rest of the story. He wiped his mouth and tasted the water. It was better than he had expected. 'No. I didn't. I think I'm past surprises now.'

Nimvar grinned, he knew that.

'The only thing I know about my father is that this medallion belonged to him.' Fizbar pulled it from a concealed pocket and held it front of Nimvar. 'It has no magical enchantment, or anything else. It's just a piece of jewellery.'

Nimvar scrunched his nose as he looked beyond the strange medallion. 'Didn't Therolius say anything?' His eyes evaded the medallion, as he knew what it represented.

'Obviously not! I'm always the last to know. My wand's not talking to me either!' Fizbar felt deflated. He scratched his stubble. 'What's he got to do with this anyway?'

Nimvar became nervous and thought to finish his story, but he felt a duty to Gildor and Fizbar.

'He's the Overlord. Surely it's part of his overseeing responsibility. Besides, he was there and he's your—'

'My what?'

'Your guardian.'

'No, he's not. He was just my teacher.'

'He's more than that, Fizbar. You may not have noticed, but he's been looking after you ever since the revolt.'

'I've always lived alone. I mean, I was raised by a group of wizards, but Therolius never showed any interest towards me. And if he did I never noticed.'

'He was there, with you, through it all. In the background.'

Fizbar was keen to press on. 'Anyway, what about Rufus?'

'Therolius rescued you from Feena. He gave you to Gimera who took you away. But there was another child on the altar, a slightly older one.'

'Just when I thought it couldn't get any worse,' said Fizbar.

'I wasn't sure at that time who it was, but we were told later that is was Geldahar.'

This time Fizbar chuckled and Nimvar thought it odd. Fizbar crossed his arms. 'Who told you?' he asked.

There was a moment's pause.

'Who told you?' asked Fizbar again, this time more rattled.

'Gimera.'

Fizbar waved his hands as if clearing the air from smoke. 'I'm a little confused. Let me think a moment.'

Fizbar thought about reaching for his wand and walking out, but this would have given the wrong impression. He also wondered why his wand was so quiet. Maybe he just didn't like hunchbacks; perhaps he was worried about being snapped in two.

'I think you've had enough information for one day.'

Nimvar thrust both hands on the table ready to help himself up, but Fizbar shot to his feet and pleaded.

'Nimvar, please. I need to know what you do. You're the only one who has been honest with me. I don't have many... Friends.'

They both sat down again slowly.

'I always knew Gimera didn't like me for some reason. My father and Therolius... I just need to put everything into perspective.'

Nimvar looked again at the journal on the table.

'Seeing Jack's life taken away was difficult to witness and Therolius's didn't react like most... Well most of us. When Rufus had finished with Jack and his father he turned to Feena on the ground. Therolius was by her side, and Rufus stood peering down at her. He ran with rage towards Therolius wand raised, but when he tried to cast a spell it didn't work. For the first time ever, his wand had refused to cast a spell at another wizard, so he was left helpless. He stood only feet from the Overlord and stared at both him and Feena, realising what had happened. No words were spoken, but glances were exchanged which said more than a thousand words. I stood behind Therolius, shocked by what had happened that night.'

Nimvar pushed a plate of food to one side and made for

the book. Fizbar grabbed it quickly and Nimvar retracted his hand without saying a word. Fizbar relaxed his grip, then his posture. Nimvar's hand was inches away from the journal. He made a fist and then pulled his hand back. Fizbar now had a better idea about his family roots, but still wondered about the journal. More questions rose in his mind, but he knew for now that the final answers had to come from the Overlord. It was time to see him again face-to-face.

'Therolius is a good wizard Fizbar, a great wizard. You should speak to him. I only hope he doesn't come looking for me.' Nimvar showed for the first time an air of concern.

'Why would he?' asked Fizbar. 'He doesn't know where you are, does he?'

'If you've asked me that, then you clearly haven't been listening? We took an oath to protect magic and uphold the reputation of wizardry. You must understand that.'

'From what you have said Therolius is the main reason for the pain and exile your race has suffered.'

'No he's not, and it's not pain. We took the oath, and the blame. We didn't like it, but we were wizards' servants, so we all felt it was our duty. Besides, we believe fully in the actions the Overlord took and we respected his power and authority.'

'Yes, but Therolius could have handled it better. After all he had nothing to hide, so why did you listen to him?

Why take the blame for something you hadn't done.'

Nimvar looked a little dismayed. He looked at Fizbar's young and sincere face. He had to tell him. 'I was Therolius's hunchback. I was the leader of the hunchbacks and had to agree with him, his decision and actions, even if I disagreed.' He fell silent.

'You were Therolius's hunchback?' Fizbar repeated.

The hunchback tilted his head. 'But there is one last thing I have to tell you.'

Fizbar looked at him expectantly.

'Therolius killed your mother.' He paused before continuing. 'He stopped her from sacrificing you. He saved your life.'

Fizbar's face changed and he oscillated between feelings of rage and gratitude. His lip trembled. His head hurt again.

'It wasn't his fault. He had to do it and nobody saw it coming. The biggest sacrifice that day is what the Overlord did and he carries that burden to this day. It's probably even greater than the one he carries about Zalbar,' said Nimvar.

'Explains why he's always in a mood,' said Fizbar, with a hint of drollness.

The hunchback nodded.

'He killed my mother,' Fizbar whispered.

'And saved your life.' Nimvar pointed at him. 'Do me one favour, wizard.'

Fizbar agreed, cautiously.

'When you confront him, ask him what he lost by killing Feena, but also what he gained.'

'What's that supposed to mean?'

'Just ask him. He'll know what I mean.'

Fizbar thought hard. 'Will we cross paths again?' the young wizard asked.

'Sooner than you think.'

Nimvar let out a large guttural bellow and Narrow Eyes entered with Plum Eyes close to his side.

'Escort the wizard to the edge of the forest. Make sure he gets there safely, understood?'

Plum Eyes was the last to concur whilst Fizbar swiftly grabbed the journal.

'What about the journal?' said Fizbar.

'All in good time, just keep it safe.'

Fizbar popped it into his cloak pocket. His approach to his wand was slower, but he grabbed it and quickly put it in his other pocket. Nimvar gave a smile, then a hiccup. Narrow Eyes was about to grab Fizbar when Nimvar spoke. 'I said escort him, I think his neck needs a rest this time, don't you?'

17

An Empty Shop

Fizbar thought long and hard about what Nimvar had told him and especially his reaction to the piece of jewellery he had yanked from his pocket. The truth about his mother's part in the revolt was unimaginable and it was obvious that Therolius should have told him. He was beginning to make sense of everything, but there were still pockets of emptiness, and only Therolius could fill those gaps. Therolius had been very evasive during his upbringing and he was unsure as to why the Overlord had chosen to hold back this information. There must have been a reason for such secrecy and Fizbar also wondered why the hunchback had chosen to reveal everything to him. It was almost as if he knew something was about to happen that would require Fizbar to have that knowledge.

He had been walking for a lengthy period, pondering and asking himself questions he couldn't find the answers to. The sky was pitch black and he approached a dark unlit roadside and stopped, pulling the journal from his pocket.

'It's not safe,' said his wand finally choosing to break his silence.

'Glad you could join me. Your silent spells are beginning to worry me. You've been distant ever since that vision in the forest.' He wondered why the wand had been silent, whilst running a hand across the journal's leather cover; feeling the complementary mix of rough and smooth textures.

'I've had a lot on my mind.' The wand sounded distant. 'What do you plan on doing now?' he asked a little more attentively.

'I don't know. I have a feeling Nimvar could have told me a lot more. I think he was a little defensive. Especially when I showed him the medallion. There's also something more to Therolius than just his evasiveness.'

'Like what?'

'I don't know, like he's hiding a bigger secret. I'm also…'

'What?'

He wet his dry lips. 'Confused why the Overlord picked me specifically. Think about it. Of all the competent wizards out there he picks a clumsy Falzard. A wizard who mucks everything up.'

'I thought you were opposed to the use of that term?'

'I am, but we have to face reality don't we?'

His wand didn't reply. A chill ran down Fizbar's spine; he knew something wasn't quite right. He felt prying eyes amongst the darkness. He began to run, swinging his arms with the journal still in hand. A white flash passed his eyes and he stumbled. His head hurt for an instant before he managed to shake the pain off and look around.

'Come on; let's get to Hetty's. Helena is in this Order of Light. I hope Hetty knows something more.'

'Then what?' asked his wand tersely.

'Then I need to see Therolius. There's more to The Grimoire than just a book.'

A yell sprang from the shadows behind him. Then silence. He turned, lifting his wand and preparing to cast a travelling spell when something shot at him knocking him over. Both his wand and journal flew from his hands and landed on the ground. As he rose from the earthy path he noticed liquid strands appearing only feet from the journal. Then a figure he knew appeared.

'You again!'

'I do have a habit of popping out of the blue, or black should I say,' said Viktor, whilst adjusting his eye patch and using his feather to light up the encounter.

Fizbar's head darted in every direction as he tried to locate the journal, but he could only see his wand very faintly, inches from him.

'Looking for this?' He waved the journal at Fizbar who slumped to the ground like a sulking child, realising that all was lost.

'Nothing? Nothing to say?' Viktor mocked with a hand

behind his ear. 'In that case I better get this back to Lord Zalbar. It's been a pleasure to make your acquaintance, Fizbar. No doubt we will see you very soon,' he added, crooning the last words before puffing into a cloud of dark threads.

Fizbar's head lifted slowly as Viktor disappeared leaving only an echoing cackle of triumph. He grabbed his wand lethargically and lifted himself off the ground. 'Told you I'm a Falzard! I can't even keep a blasted book safe!' He looked at his spoon. 'Yeah, knew you'd be quiet again,' he added.

Therolius wasn't going to be happy. Fizbar was used to disappointment and resentment, it was part of being a Falzard, but what really annoyed him was the simple fact that he couldn't guard or protect a book. It wasn't a tall order and he had dealt with bigger tasks before, like the recent dragon escapade. Whichever way he looked at it, he still ended up thinking about the humiliation and his lack of ability. Surely this would hinder any chance of advancing up the wizarding ladder. Surely his career as a wizard was about to come to an end, just as it was getting started. Putting aside further introspection he clenched his wand, and then cast a spell.

A blue light burst from the dark night and Fizbar landed in a wagon of hay across the street from The Magic Garden. Blades of dried grass tickled him whilst he slid to the bottom, then off the end. He brushed the hay from his garments and spat without aim, removing straw from his mouth whilst fixing his attention on the shop. He noticed that the door was open but the lights were out. He walked across the road with caution, and with his wand ready and leading the way.

The night was still and Fizbar's senses intensified as he stepped through the doorway. The bell did not ring this time. It appeared to be frozen, pointing towards the ceiling. Then the silence was broken as sniffles surfaced from behind the shop counter. As Fizbar approached watchfully, the sniffling increased. He peered over the worktop and saw Hetty on the floor leaning against a bookcase, clutching a tissue in one hand and a gold medallion in the other.

'Hetty,' said Fizbar softly, careful not to shock or startle her.

She looked up, the moonlight piercing the window and lighting up her face. Her watery eyes glistened, and a single tear sparkled as it trickled down her cheek. 'I can't find her.' Hetty sniffed, and then wiped her cheek embarrassed about her appearance.

'Who? Helena?'

Hetty nodded.

'Are you all right?' He crouched down beside her.

She shrugged.

'Where's Helena?'

Hetty shrugged again.

'What happened here?' asked Fizbar as he glanced around the room noticing the destruction.

'The Lex Talionis.' She sniffed again, and then blew her nose loudly.

'Seems I'm not the only one who can trash the place,' said Fizbar trying to cheer her up, but it didn't work. 'How do you know it was the Lex?'

'People saw the Hex twins and a one-eyed pirate.'

Fizbar thought, *Viktor*.

'And a goat.' She wiped her eyes. 'For heaven's sake, why would a goat be involved? I thought fauns were pretty and cuddly, and now I just want to eat one!' she said in a trembling, upset and slightly manic tone.

'I guess there is evil in everyone and everything,' said Fizbar, fearing he'd said another wrong thing, but Hetty smiled and looked up at him.

Fizbar looked baffled, but he knew why they had come. He wiped her cheek. 'Helena had a journal didn't she?'

'I don't know.' Her voice still trembled. For a moment she thought hard. 'Yes, a small brown book. She always kept it close to her. Just like this medallion.' She raised it high, but Fizbar had already noticed it. 'It's a round earth medallion. Rare and only found in expensive antique stalls,' Hetty explained. Its design included convoluted spirals and the pattern was like a crazy stained-glass window, but without the glass; just the golden struts. It hung on a long thick gold chain.

Fizbar pulled an identical medallion from his tunic.

Hetty smiled affectedly. 'Well, I guess it's not that rare then. That makes me feel so much better.' There was a hint of sarcasm in her voice.

'It was the only thing my father left me.' He looked at his, then Hetty's. 'They're the same.'

Hetty analysed them both for any distinctive differences. 'You're right. It's highly unlikely you'd get two with the same convolutions unless…'

They both looked in amazement.

'Unless there was a mould,' said Fizbar.

Hetty resisted, but forced her words out. 'I was going to suggest that they were at an affectionate point in their lives.'

Fizbar looked lost.

'Unless they were in love…' Hetty made it clear.

There was a moment's pause before Fizbar grunted and changed the subject, although this suggestion served to join up the questions at the back of his mind. Maybe his father had betrayed his mother, he thought. That would explain her actions. Could this have been the reason she turned on the Order and her friends and family; and on him? Did it push her over the edge? His thoughts ran wild.

'My mother never talked of anyone other than my father.'

Fizbar's eyes lit up. 'What was his name?'

'Marcus Elantari. He was a normal person, I mean not

magical, a herbalist. My mother said I got my love of herbology from him.'

Fizbar felt warmth in her words; he felt better and his mood lifted. He tucked the medallion back under his garments. 'The journal, where is it?'

'I don't know, with her I suppose.' The young herbalist dabbed her eyes with the tissue.

'I think a visit to Therolius is in order.'

'My mother always told me to see Gimera in times of peril. I think this counts as peril doesn't it?'

'I suppose so, but I still think we should see the Overlord.'

They both ran from the shop and the door creaked. This time the bell rang as the door shut.

18

Heritage

Hetty and Fizbar ran down a narrow lane, hand in hand, Fizbar thinking about what to say to the Overlord and Hetty worried about her mother. They arrived at a tall block that was on the opposite side to the school grounds. They couldn't see the top windows, as the block seemed to vanish as it towered into the sky. There was a strange swirling in the night sky as clouds moved, preventing the stars from gazing down. Fizbar and Hetty anticipated each other's moves, as they were both about to knock on the solid black door.

'Psst!'

'Did you hear that?' Fizbar asked Hetty.

'No.'

'Psst! Over here!'

Hetty stepped off the doorstep and zoomed into the darkness after hearing it for the first time, and then a man came into the foreground behaving erratically. It was Gildor.

'Please. You have to come with me. We don't have much time.'

'Gildor, how did you get away from the Arctodi?'

'There's one good reason to breed Granther's you know, Fizbar.'

'We're here to see Gimera. He'll know what to do. Hetty's mother told her that...'

'I know, and that's why you have to come with me.'

'What do you mean you know?' asked Hetty.

'I'll explain, but first you have to come with me. Before *he* comes out.' He jabbed at the tall building, as the lights began to switch off one by one. 'Quick, he's coming.'

Fizbar and Hetty looked at him cautiously; still fixed in their position and unwilling to comply. Gildor looked around, whilst wiping his sweaty forehead with a handkerchief.

'It'd better be a good reason,' said Fizbar.

'I assure you it is. There are things you don't know, and suspicions that are now confirmed.'

The last light went out and the door rattled. They both ran to the edge of Gimera's building and entered a narrow alleyway. They peered round the corner as the door opened. Gimera appeared and his long red cloak lifted as he locked his front door with a watchful eye. Then he raised an exquisite piece of twirling wood, his wand, and vanished.

As they walked towards the end of the alley, night-lamps lit up in sequence, illuminating the lane. A few passers by shot suspicious glances at Gildor, and he was fully aware of their curiosity.

'What was all that, Gildor? Gimera needs to know about Helena—'

'Like I said, I know everything and Gimera is the last person you should talk to.'

'If there is any hostility between you and the Archmage, now is not the time,' said Fizbar, looking for agreement from Hetty.

'It has nothing to do with any hostility on my part; this has more to do with you.'

'I don't want any more surprises, Gildor; so then let's go to Therolius. He'll—'

'He's not there either.' Gildor interjected.

'You better start speaking clearly, Gildor. We are both struggling to understand what's going on.'

'All right,' Gildor stooped a little, 'what do you know about the Order of the Light?' he asked.

Hetty shrugged. She'd never heard of it.

'What did Nimvar say? Did he explain everything?'

'Who's Nimvar?' Hetty asked.

'He's a hunchback,' said Gildor.

She looked disconcerted.

'Yes, he told me quite a bit.'

'Anything particularly important?'

Fizbar started counting on his fingers. 'He told me

about my mother, her attempt to sacrifice me, about my father, an uprising…'

'And?'

'Isn't that enough already?' Hetty butted in.

Fizbar thought hard. 'He suggested that Therolius was my guardian, supposedly.'

'And?'

'You mean there's more!' Hetty added rolling her eyes.

'My mother's involvement with Zalbar's father.'

'Well, I never! Just when I thought it couldn't get any worse,' Hetty blurted out.

'Now you know how I feel,' replied Fizbar, noticing a smile creep onto Hetty's delicate features.

'Anything more?' asked Gildor.

'That Therolius caused the revolt.'

They both looked at Hetty who gestured zipping her mouth, and then placed her hands on her hips.

'That's not entirely true. Maybe that's where his story was a little wayward.' Gildor rubbed his chin, his other hand in a pocket of a dull brownish-yellow tweed suit that fitted him well. The red tie looked slightly odd, but after all peculiarity was Gildor's specialty. 'I was there also, at the revolt,' he added.

'Nimvar said you and Gimera tried to contain my mother despite her aptitude.'

'She was losing control. It needed diplomatic intervention.'

'He said something to that effect.'

'I'm still a little lost. Why couldn't we see Gimera and tell him everything? After all he is the Archmage,' asked Hetty.

'Let me ask you a question. Why do you think crime is getting worse by the week here in Sintar?' He waited patiently for a response.

'There's more bad people being born?' She waved her hand in the air without cause. Fizbar thinking it to be a genuine reply, nodded in agreement.

'The Archmage is the next in line for the position of Overlord. Isn't it odd that he allows crime to become rife seeing as it's his responsibility to stop and control it?'

'Gildor has a point. He does work for the Council,' Fizbar said to Hetty.

'Especially giving you a level three job with that dragon, it should never have happened.'

'Level three!' Fizbar raised his voice. 'I should be a level three?'

'Forget that, what I'm trying to say is that you shouldn't have been allocated that task in the first place. Doesn't that raise any alarm bells?'

Fizbar thought about an appropriate answer, but couldn't think of anything. 'Maybe he wants to get rid of you?'

Gildor rolled his hands, in hope that Fizbar would catch on.

'That's absurd! Why would he do that? What threat could I pose to him or the Council?'

'Finally, you're getting warmer.'

'I'm still lost,' said Hetty looking around. 'I'm also a little cold.'

Fizbar took off his cloak, for the first time revealing his scrawny build, and wrapped it around her. Hetty didn't mind, she thought him sweet. His hat was still stuck to his head, and a little lopsided.

'*Gimera is working for Zalbar*,' whispered Gildor.

Fizbar was left open-mouthed; although Gildor was amazed he hadn't caught on sooner.

'How do you know this?' Hetty asked the question that was dancing in Fizbar's mind.

'My suspicion started the day of the revolt. Therolius gave Gimera Feena's journal. It had notes of binding spells, attempts at merging magic with the physical form. It must have been very tempting for a wizard of his ability to attempt that. Curiosity is a powerful trap for wizards. Inquisitive behaviour and a desire to explore is what drives us towards excellence.'

'I suppose the same can be said about everyone,' Hetty added and Gildor agreed.

'You mentioned Gimera in your shack; that's what you were referring to wasn't it?' Fizbar asked.

Gildor approached Fizbar invading his personal space. 'Therolius gave you Geldahar's notebook. You know it's a binding journal?'

'Yes.'

'Do you know *how* he managed to make a binding journal?'

Fizbar shook his head. Hetty's expression remained blank.

'With your mother's notes. He used her failures and perfected them.'

'How did he get my mother's jou— Ohhh!' he suddenly realised.

'Yes, Gimera was working with him from the start. It was Gimera who encouraged Zalbar. He handed him your mother's journal. He recognised his potential and made him what he is now. It wasn't Therolius's fault. None of it was.'

'Then why is he so full of remorse?' Fizbar asked.

'It's a trait in the best of us. He lost someone very dear to him that day.'

'Who?'

'Your father.'

Fizbar looked confused. 'My father?'

'Yes. Jack.'

'What do you mean?'

'Jack, your father—'

'Yes what?' Fizbar cut in.

Gildor realised that Nimvar hadn't told him everything.

'What?' Fizbar pressed.

Gildor took a deep breath. 'Jack was Therolius's son.'

Hetty's eyes nearly popped from their sockets. Fizbar titled his head back as if the final piece of the puzzle had been connected.

'That makes Therolius your grandfather,' said Hetty.

Lightheaded, Fizbar sat down on a small wall. He kicked a can that spun away across the floor and he rested his hands on his knees. 'I knew there was more to this.' After a few seconds he frowned and then asked the obvious question. 'Hang on! We have different surnames, so how is it possible? It makes no sense.'

'It's an anagram,' said Hetty as she took off the cloak and wrapped it around Fizbar. 'I think you need this more than me now.'

'She's right. DELRUNT is TRUNDLE,' Gildor pointed out.

'I don't understand.' Fizbar didn't know what else to say, his head felt heavy as all the pieces of information began clicking together.

'When Jack was young, very young, Therolius and his wife Astra lived in Fintar. That's when the Order of Light was created. To set up a secret guild to protect magic. Crime was rife in Fintar and Therolius was Archmage. He ordered a magical police to be formed to control malevolence in Fintar as the public were beginning to distrust wizards and their ability to preserve order. For some reason, this didn't go down well with the Council so he was sent to Sintar.'

'But he is the Overlord. Why did they promote him?' asked Fizbar.

'The last Overlord died suddenly. There were rumours that Gimera was involved in a conspiracy, but it was never proved and the rumours were silenced almost as quickly as they started. He was also sent to Sintar. There was no-one to promote, and nobody worthy of the post, but bloodlines rule in the wizarding world. Therolius was made Overlord and Gimera became the Archmage much later.'

'So Therolius promoted Gimera?'

'I know it sounds silly, but what better way to keep your eye on him. You know the saying, keep your friends close and your enemies' closer.'

'I can't think straight, Gildor. This is just too much to absorb,' said Fizbar.

'I know it must be hard, but it will all seem clear in the morning.'

'I'm not so sure. It's hard for me and I'm not involved,' said Hetty.

'We should make a move. I think I know where Therolius is.'

They set off and the streets were quiet and still. Gildor had his wand out and ready, and Hetty clutched Fizbar's hand firmly. He felt a certain tenderness and sensed a fondness forming; but for now he was more concerned about his heritage. He whispered to himself and Hetty overhearing him, smiled. *Fizbar Delrunt... Fizbar Delrunt... FD.*

19

The Pure-Blood

Three knocks on the door and no reply. The three of them glanced at each other with tensed expressions. Gildor knocked again. Still no answer. He turned the door handle. It was unlocked. The door creaked open and Gildor squeezed his button-like face through the opening, his small eyes darting erratically. He couldn't see anyone or anything moving which was a clear indication that the office was empty. He pushed the door open wide and the others followed close behind him. Hetty had never been in an Overlord's office before. In astonishment she approached the many shelves full of intricate objects, running her fingers through some of the old manuscripts, and picking up old books and odd jars. This included a primer of herbs that was very dear and familiar to her, and a volume that had aided in her herbology studies. The contents on the shelves made her smile with warmth. 'Fascinating!' Hetty summed it up in one word, whilst moving her fingers gently across alchemic beakers, strangely shaped bottles and long rubber tubes, before stopping at a shelf of strange plants. 'I know what these are...'

Gildor ignored her. So did Fizbar. Something strange began to occur. The young wizard felt an instant pull towards a large door as if lassoed around the waist. The door was just six feet in front of him and a subtle green flicker shone from its base. Reluctantly, he was pulled closer and closer, whilst Hetty and Gildor were preoccupied. Gildor searched the Overlord's desk drawers in hope of finding a clue to his whereabouts. The bottom drawer was locked and Gildor cast a spell to open it. Inside was nothing of interest. It was full of student's exam papers, mostly unmarked. He searched under the desk, but still nothing. Then he moved to the window and looked down at the street below as if searching for a lost item, when in reality he was hoping Therolius would turn the corner any minute and head up to the school. He turned and glanced back at Fizbar with a question on the tip of his tongue, but was cut short by Fizbar's strange movements.

Fizbar pointed. 'What's in there?'

Gildor followed his eyes right down to his finger, and then shot to the foot of the door. He noticed the glow and ran in front of him with a fast and erratic rant. 'You can't go in there, it's forbidden. You just can't. Therolius will be mad if you enter there. Only he can enter that room.'

'Why? What's so important?' He pressed Gildor to

reply with the truth.

Fizbar was transfixed by the green light. He stepped forwards, but Gildor stood his ground. The radiance grew with every step, now seeping from the gaps around the door frame. With every pace forward by Fizbar the light intensified until even Hetty turned to see where the light was coming from.

'It's that famed green glow.' Hetty spoke out in a calm tone. She knew what it was almost immediately. 'That's the room that has…'

'Yes, The Grimoire! It's in that room, but as I said, only Therolius is allowed in there.'

'Yes, but he's not here is he?' said Fizbar, as droplets of sweat began to form on Gildor's forehead. He took a deep breath. 'What you need is not in that room. We must find the Overlord.'

'Maybe the answer lies in there,' Fizbar suggested.

'I'm not sure it's a good idea to tamper with what you don't understand. Maybe Gildor's right,' Hetty added.

'Hoorah! Precisely young Elantiel. Listen to her. She's wiser than she looks!'

'But then again maybe Fizbar's right,' she shot back at Gildor.

'I take it all back!' Gildor turned to the window with both hands on the windowsill.

'Do you really think the answer lies in there, Fizbar?' Hetty asked.

'There's only one way to find out.' Fizbar moved towards the door.

Gildor started to bite his nails like a mad man. He scrunched his face and pushed his glasses back, but the sweat just made them slide down to the end of his nose. 'Besides, you need a special key to get in there. Only the Overlord has it. I really think we should focus on finding Therolius and Helena…'

Fizbar suddenly remembered and dipped into his pocket. He pulled out a strange key.

'Oh great! He's got the key!' Gildor turned away, too horrified to look any further. 'If only things couldn't get any worse.'

'Therolius gave this to me when he handed me the journal' He approached with a cautious hand. 'The Overlord's key. Maybe this is what he wanted me to guard instead of the book.' He thought hard trying to make sense of it all.

'The Grimoire. Imagine that!' Hetty was already amazed. She'd never been in the school of magic as only blue-bloods and wizards were allowed here. Fizbar's hand started to tremble as he lowered the key into the keyhole. He could now feel the pressure. He heard a clunk, and turned it.

A vivid ray of green light jumped into the room. Fizbar looked at both Gildor and Hetty as he entered, whilst shielding his eyes. Gildor still wasn't happy, but he thought that if Therolius had given Fizbar the key, he must have had a good reason for doing so. As Fizbar entered the light changed to a serene golden glow.

'Impossible!' shouted Gildor, 'It's can't be,' he exclaimed in shock.

'What?' Hetty urged an answer. 'What's wrong?'

'Therolius… He knew… All along, he knew!' Gildor added in delight.

'What? Will you tell me what's going on?'

Fizbar walked through the door. The room was small but seemed the right size for him. Mounted on the shiny brass moulded lectern was The Grimoire. The large and ornamental leather cover glowed a light shade of yellow. The four small pearls at each corner shone a violent gold. Fizbar approached it and was anxious to touch it, but instinctively restrained his hand. He attempted three times more before finally plucking up the courage. As he did, the golden aura engulfed him. Visions filled his mind. The revolt. He saw it. The hunchbacks, the wizards, and the riot. Hunchback's dropped like petals from a flower. Wizards fell too. He felt the pain and anguish. He was there. The suffering was unbearable; the visions dug at his mind. He tried to remove his hand but couldn't and started to scream. Faces, many faces flashed before his eyes until he was left with only one. A face he had never seen before. The three shiny brass clasps flung open, the pain vanished, and so did the face. All was quiet for a few seconds, then he could hear Hetty shouting his name as a distant echo. He picked up The Grimoire and feeling dizzy left the room. As he re-entered the Overlord's office Gildor had his hands covering his face. He prized open his fingers so he could see, frightened at what might appear before him. Then he removed all his fingers and he ran to Fizbar and hugged him in relief. The Falzard smiled, but urged Gildor to relent a little as he was squeezing Fizbar too hard.

'You're a pure-blood! Therolius knew!'

'Is that facial expression revealing shock because you're surprised, or because I'm a Falzard? Besides, I can't be,' said Fizbar with an edge of enquiry in his tone.

'Let me just assure you that I've also never been partial to class distinction, as far as I am concerned a wizard is a wizard whatever his wand may be.'

'Or hers!' Hetty added glancing at Fizbar for a brief moment before darting over to him. She didn't know whether to embrace him or not. Gildor smiled. His expression was assuring, but still Hetty held back, containing her delight.

'Therolius said that a pure blood has to be proven and sanctioned by the book. It's not entirely down to blood type,' said Fizbar staring at Hetty. 'It's all right.' Fizbar felt a warm glow. 'I know where Therolius is.' He looked at Gildor and then into Hetty's eyes. 'And your mother is there with him.'

'Helena and Therolius... Please. I'm sure that's not true. Therolius is not her type.' She declared in disapproval.

Fizbar tutted. 'Not like that. I saw it. Zalbar has them at the forest and we need to get there quickly.'

Hetty's disapproval vanished and was replaced by horror.

'How do you know? Was it The Grimoire?' Gildor asked.

'I saw images, many visions both past and present, some I don't even understand. What I do know is that they're at the forest... Where it all began.'

'Are they alive?'

'I hope so, but don't get too comfortable. I think Zalbar has all the journals.'

'Then he needs a sacrifice if he plans to repeat...' Gildor stopped short.

'What my mother attempted many years ago.' Fizbar finished the sentence in shame. He looked down at the glowing Grimoire in his hands. 'I need to take this with me.'

'The book should stay here in the school. It's the only protection it has.' Gildor was adamant.

'Therolius didn't protect the book like most have believed, even the Order I suppose.'

'Yes he did! He cast a spell to protect it,' Gildor insisted.

'That's what he said, but the book didn't have a spell. The book simply protects itself.'

'But Zalbar…'

'He simply wasn't a pure blood. I imagine Therolius made that story up. We know he's good at keeping secrets from the best of us.'

Gildor laughed in agreement. 'So how do we stop Zalbar from performing the incantation? I assume that's why he's at the forest. If he had Therolius and Helena then he must have all the journals.'

'I'm not sure. All I know is that we need to get to the forest.'

'What do you plan to do?' Hetty asked.

'Again, I don't know,' said Fizbar glaring at the book. 'I'm sure Therolius has let his guard down a second time. One of his faults is that he thinks everybody is redeemable.'

'A quality an Overlord should possess,' Gildor added firmly.

'So how do we get there in time?' Fizbar asked.

'Now there I can help,' Hetty exclaimed. 'We can whizz there.'

'The forest is a long way away for travel spells. I hope you're not suggesting we use The Grimoire?' said Gildor with a slight edge to his voice.

'No. I was recently at Frangar's swamp collecting samples and I know of a location that will enable the second journey. I believe that is possible.'

'Yes. If we have stable ground to land on, we can set off again. The shortest path to the forest is through the swamp.'

Gildor didn't like the sound of this and wasn't convinced. 'Many wizards have died trying to make a landing there, you know where it gets its name from.'

'Yes, yes, yes. I had this discussion with my mother. The more important question is can you do it?' she asked, wide-eyed and waiting for a response.

'They call that place Frangar's step.'

'I know. Can you land there or not?' She was starting to lose her self-control.

Gildor didn't reply, but he appeared to be nodding.

'Is that a yes?'

'It's dangerous. I'm not sure for myself let alone the responsibility of two other people.'

'I'm not your responsibility, Gildor.'

There was a split-second before Fizbar declared: 'I can do it.' He thought hard again. *I can do it.*

Both Gildor and Hetty objected in unison.

'I don't think that's wise, Master. You've never—'

'You've been quiet for a while, so keep it that way,' said Fizbar sourly to his wand.

'I was only—'

'Well don't!' He seemed upset for some reason. 'I can do this. I wouldn't suggest it if I couldn't.'

The others looked on with a mixture of awe and scepticism.

'Besides… I have The Grimoire, what could possibly

go wrong?'

The statement didn't make either of them more comfortable as they looked at each other for reassurance.

'Do you know the spot, Fizbar?' Gildor asked.

'I've been there once, if that's what you are asking. Why would I suggest such a thing, if I'd never even been there?'

Gildor acquiesced. 'We'll need to do it quickly then, so Fizbar will do the first journey. As soon as we touch down, I'll be ready to get us out again.'

Shaking their heads nervously they all agreed. Hetty wrapped her arms around Fizbar. This made him nervous. She could sense his unease, but also something else. She smiled. Gildor grabbed Fizbar and they all huddled as though they were trying to conserve their body heat. Fizbar lifted his wand.

'Remember carefully, visualise the spot and you'll have no problem. Just like you've done in class,' said Gildor.

Fizbar felt as if he were back at school, memories of his practicals flashed back. This was what he had trained for. This was reality. This was survival.

'*Itio Franger!*' shouted Fizbar and a swirl of grey cloud circled the three of them like a mini tornado. Papers flew around the office and the table even moved across the floor. The force increased. Time slowed as Fizbar thought hard about the meaning of everything including his being a pure-blood. How was that possible? The Grimoire slipped a little in his hand and the thoughts left his mind as he opened his eyes through the howling wind. Then they all vanished. Suddenly they appeared in the swamp. Gildor looked down and noticed they were hovering over a bubbling body of water, a little short of the hammock know as Franger's step. He reacted with precision and rapidity with, '*Itio rapidito Filtzer!*' They disappeared a second time and just as quickly they reappeared.

20

The Final Blow?

A bright bolt of white light filled the night air, as they landed on dry ground. Fizbar lifted himself up from the prone position in which he'd landed, brushed his cloak and straightened his hat. He felt jittery as adrenaline pumped through his body and he had a sick feeling in his stomach. As he brushed his hand over the Grimoire, he noticed the aura had vanished and he wondered why. Now it was just as normal as any other large leather book and it was heavy. He looked around at the thick trees and large clumps of stone; then as a cold damp air rushed past him he sped off without hesitation.

'That was close!' said Hetty in a quivering tone, whilst Gildor straightened his back as an old duelling injury began playing up.

'Just as well there were two of us wouldn't you say Master Trundle?' said Gildor with a hint of admiration. After all, no wizard let alone a Falzard had ever managed the Frangar step. He pushed his glasses back up the bridge of his nose and searched for Fizbar. Hetty tidied her hair, and he caught a glimpse of the young wizard running towards the forest edge as fast as his skinny legs could carry him. Fizbar's body ached and he felt weary both physically and mentally. The thought in his mind troubled him, *Therolius, my grandfather!* A surprise that he wasn't sure he truly believed. Zalbar had managed to trap the Overlord somehow and it was Fizbar's duty as a wizard first to serve and protect. Then he could begin an inquisition into the Delrunt family tree.

'Come on!' Gildor shrieked before grabbing Hetty's hand, and yanking her on. His concentration was intense as he crossed the leafy terrain in his tweed suit. His black and white brogues were full of mud, which made them seem heavier with each step and they pulled at his knees; however he didn't protest. Hetty lagged a little behind. She found it difficult to run in her tightly fitted skirt. She looked like a dancer with her arms performing graceful manoeuvres as she clambered over the uneven ground. Regardless of their potential peril, they managed to press on, and Fizbar was well ahead. His wand still chose silence and he resisted the temptation to ask it the questions circling in his mind. The spoon really had been quiet and Fizbar began to realise something was wrong. Most times he couldn't keep his wand from spouting suggestions about the smallest detail. There was something further that worried him, something he had seen back at the school.

He brushed his pondering aside as he came to a bushy patch. He stopped and waited for the others to arrive.

'It's not much further.' Fizbar lowered his voice, moving branches from his face as he advanced through the vegetation. A branch tugged at his hat, but he managed to break it free. The air was sharp. The night pitch black. The only audible sounds were the "twit-t-wooing" of owls and the "tonk" sounds of frogs.

'I can't see very well, Fizbar. Light your wand,' whispered Hetty as she moved closer towards him, clutching his robe.

'No. They'll see us,' he replied in a hushed voice.

'Who?'

'Them!' He pointed through a small clearing at three dark cloaked figures. Small white lights shone from the tips of their wands illuminating the front of a large tent. They appeared to be guarding the tent, panning around for possible threats. 'Zalbar must be close,' he added as steam lifted from his lips into the cold air.

'Is he in there?' asked Hetty.

'No. He must be at the sacrificial altar.'

'Then who's in there?' Hetty's face was blank. She looked at Gildor who was sweating profusely. 'Do you know?'

Suddenly the large black flap of the tent opened. Two Lex Talionis appeared, and then held up the flap for the last to exit. A figure dressed in a red cloak signalled to the others to follow. The small cap that sat on his head was, like the red cloak, unmistakable. Fizbar and Gildor exchanged looks, and then sighed with disappointment.

'Traitor!' whispered Gildor in anger, scrunching his eyes. He didn't need his glasses to identify betrayal. 'I'll never get used to it!'

Gimera the Archmage left with a hurried motion. When they were out of earshot, Fizbar raised two fingers to his eyes, then in the direction of the Archmage. 'Follow closely, but we must keep our distance. If we raise any suspicion… It's all over.'

Gimera and his men continued down a wild path that coiled towards the lake. Fizbar knew exactly where they were going. It was ten minutes before the sacrificial altar came into view. It was surrounded by many candles with flames dancing and flickering with the night air.

'The ritual. It must have started,' said Gildor. 'We're too late.' He slumped his shoulders.

'Look,' Hetty pointed. 'Hunchbacks.' She noticed them closing in from the distance all carrying lit torches. A few had already arrived at the altar. 'What are you going to do Fizbar?' she asked hurriedly. 'The book… It's not glowing. Is it broken?'

Fizbar kept one eye on the book and the other on Gimera who had now approached the foot of the altar. His cronies close behind him turned and joined the rest on the Lex Talionis who were guarding the altar. He could see two others. Someone leaning over the altar in a frozen state, and another lying on it. 'I don't think so... I'm not sure, but there is only one way to find out.'

He moved closer as the rest followed, anxious, scared and uncertain of what was to come. As they got closer they could see Zalbar bending over the body on the altar. Hetty identified her mother lying flat and motionless. She was about to rush out, but both Gildor and Fizbar restrained her, each grabbing a wrist.

'But it's my mother!' she said quietly, and tearfully, although she looked outraged. 'I have to do something.'

'I know, and we will,' Fizbar whispered back. 'But I have to go alone. I've got to face Zalbar alone.'

'That's suicide!' Gildor pointed out. 'You might as well admit defeat now,' he added through gritted teeth.

'Is that all the encouragement I get?' Fizbar asked, his face pale as chalk. Gildor didn't make a response and just folded his arms. 'It's the only way. I have to confront him.'

'He'll kill you. He's too powerful for you. Hell! He's too powerful for me,' said Gildor, knowing that this would give him the encouragement he needed. 'Even the wizards of the Order wouldn't attempt a confrontation.' Then even he started to believe what he was saying to Fizbar. He was scared; Zalbar *was* too powerful for him.

'That figures, where is the Order when you need them the most!' said Fizbar with a hint of sarcasm, even though he had been imagining the horrors of Zalbar's mastery.

'I'm here aren't I?'

Fizbar stared blankly at Gildor's round face; his rosy cheeks the size of apples. He twisted his lips, attempting a smile. 'I know Gildor… I know you are,' both hands gripped the book. 'But I have The Grimoire, what could possibly go wrong?'

'If I listed all the possibilities, we'd be here all night,' said Gildor whilst brushing his tweed waistcoat, checking his buttons in a nervous manner. A pink nose complemented the rest of his rosy complexion.

'I've been thinking…' Fizbar raised the book out in front of them. All eyes shot to the cover. 'If Zalbar has the journals and I have The Grimoire, surely I should have more power than him? Or the same at the very least.'

'It depends what you mean by power. It's difficult to separate and explain. If we look…' Gildor started to explain.

'This is no time for a lecture, Gildor. Besides, the book is broken,' Hetty cut in, fiddling with a twig. 'It's not glowing anymore.'

'It's not broken. It can't break,' Gildor assured her, and then hesitated. 'It's because we took it out of the school.'

'What's that got to do with it?' Hetty asked.

'It's the only logical explanation I can think of.' He started to pace in small circles. 'The book has never been out of the school. Maybe it has no power outside the Overlord's quarters.'

'Have you forgotten Gelorg!' Fizbar interjected, testing Gildor.

'What?'

'Remember Gelorg, the story about—'

'I know the story very well, Fizbar.'

'Nimvar told me it's one of many falsities. A lie to protect The Grimoire.'

'If you're so clever, then why haven't you realised that Gelorg never even existed.'

Fizbar turned to confront the red-faced teacher. Even Hetty looked just as bewildered as he felt. 'What do you mean?'

Hetty didn't say a word, just like Fizbar's wand.

'Gelorg is Gimera. He stole the book once, but Therolius managed to stop him. Why do you think he's working for Zalbar? He was aware of Gimera's evil tendencies, so it must have been easy to employ his services.'

'Gimera, I…'

'The story just keeps getting better doesn't it?' said Hetty.

Both shot her a sharp look. A twig snapped and instinctively they all ducked. Fizbar peered ahead and saw Zalbar talking to another figure. It was Therolius, but he wasn't moving.

'Well Overlord, it's just about that time.' Zalbar rested his staff next to Helena's thigh and rolled up his sleeves revealing his skeletal hands. 'Time to start this ritual. Any last words?' He put his ear close to Therolius's mouth. 'Nothing to say? I thought as much.'

'I'm going, Therolius needs me.' Fizbar got to his feet, trembling, but Gildor grabbed his shoulder.

'No dear boy, were in this together!'

Hetty gave Fizbar a look that said quite plainly: 'I'm scared.'

'I'm scared to,' he said, and smiled warmly at her.

'All right, Gildor. But Hetty stay's here. This is a wizard's thing.'

Hetty didn't answer, and she didn't look him in the eye.

'Please Hetty, say you'll stay here.' He touched her cheek, moving her face to meet his. 'Please, it's too dangerous.'

Reluctantly she nodded, as her wet eyes glistened at him. Gildor was keeping an eye on the Lex Talionis. They moved closer. Fizbar grabbed a branch and leaned on it making sure his view was clear. He noticed Therolius bending over the altar, and knew a spell was preventing him from moving. It was still too far away to see their faces. Gimera waltzed over to Zalbar and handed him a book.

'I think he has all the journals. That must have been the last one,' said Gildor.

'What do you mean?'

'I imagine the last journal he's handed over belonged to your mother.'

Fizbar tried to locate the book, but was drawn away by Zalbar's laughter. He felt furious and decided that now was the time to wipe that invisible smile off Zalbar's empty face. He forced The Grimoire into the back of his trousers, covering it with his cloak. It felt cold, but he didn't flinch. He swallowed hard and closed his eyes for a moment's composure, before mustering the courage to dash out in front of the Lex Talionis. They drew their wands immediately they saw Fizbar and Gildor approaching.

'ZALBAR!' Fizbar shouted, panting a little.

Gildor rushed to his side. Both had their wands at the ready. Three of the Lex met them, blocking their advance.

'It's all right... Let them through,' Gimera said in a condescending tone. 'They won't be leaving.'

The Lex pulled to one side letting them both brush past. Fizbar's eyes met those of the Hex brothers and Viktor. The faun stuck out its pink tongue at them, and then spat at Gildor. He pulled out a handkerchief, and with an upturned nose wiped the green viscosity from his face.

Zalbar swivelled round and greeted them, his hands preoccupied with rearranging the journals, placing them in order. 'Ah! Master Trundle and...' he dipped his head. 'GILDOR! My friends, what a lovely surprise.'

'We're no friends of yours!' Fizbar shot back firmly. 'And I can assure you, it's no surprise for us.' They took another couple of paces forward. They were at least ten feet from the altar. 'We are here to take Therolius and

Helena home,' Fizbar added.

'Really?' Zalbar replied without hesitation; then he sighed heavily. Fizbar noticed his wand stuck to his skeletal hand. 'A Falzard and a petty washed up teacher?'

A little smile twisted Gimera's face; his body puffed up.

'You know the Order of Light is headed by Gimera?' He flicked a skeletal finger at the Archmage, left the journals, and glided a few paces closer. 'There is *no* Order of Light,' he added, his arms out as if he was about to cure an ill person.

'We don't need the Order,' Fizbar replied without looking at Gildor. He noticed his hands were trembling. 'Isn't that right Gildor?' Gildor nodded like a child who had been told off.

Zalbar laughed again. 'That's just as well then. They have failed to protect The Grimoire, and magic itself. Now I will be the ruler of Sintar and the rest of the world, I might add. When I become the supreme wizard, you will have no use for that spoon you carry around with you. So what will you do with yourself?' He bent an elbow supporting his other arm; his finger touched his chin. He appeared deep in thought, but it only lasted for a second. 'Oh! That's right; you'll be serving me, along with the rest of the wizards. They will be my new hunchbacks.'

Meedril the hunchback stood with a torch in hand close to the sacrificial altar. He didn't like the sound of Zalbar's announcement. He wiped his nose and noticed the staff beside Helena. Fizbar shot a questioning look at Meedril who shied from his gaze. He was surprised at the hunchback's choice of master, but was also disappointed as he expected a little honour amongst associates. After all, it wasn't long ago he had helped him out with the Korrigans. He sighed, and twisted his hips a little because The Grimoire was digging into his back.

'You don't have The Grimoire,' Fizbar shortened Zalbar's laugh. 'You'll never rule Sintar. Therolius does.' He pointed to the lifeless Overlord.

'Who? Him?' Zalbar circled the Overlord. Therolius's eyes followed him. 'Is that true Therolius? Going to save the world? Put all the wrongs to right? Even your wrongs?' He stopped and straightened himself. 'I DON'T THINK SO!' He shouted and then floated back to the altar. 'Don't you know anything boy? Or should I address you differently?' He waited for a response from Fizbar. 'No? Nothing? Well, the journals are all I need. I have perfected the incantation your mother got so very wrong.'

'It wasn't my mother's fault. She was ill,' Fizbar replied, anger in his voice.

'Well, that's one way of summing her up I suppose.'

Fizbar lifted his spoon, pointing at Zalbar's void of a face. 'You'd better explain yourself why you still have the chance!'

Zalbar acted afraid. 'Please, don't point the spoon at me. I'll give you what you want. I'll set them all free.' He laughed and turned, moving back to the stone altar. 'Do you know everything about your mother, Falzard?'

'I know everything I need to know about her.'

'About her and my father?'

'Yes.' His nose turned with disgust. 'I heard there was an... An...'

'Affection involved?'

'I wouldn't call it that.'

'So obviously Therolius told you about us then?'

Fizbar's heart beat faster at the swirling strands in Zalbar's void. If he had had a face, he was sure a grin would be spreading over it right about now. 'What do you mean, *us*? There *is* no us!' he said sharply.

'Well, well, well. It seems as though something has slipped your mind... Little brother!'

Fizbar turned his ear; he thought he must have misunderstood.

'Cat got your tongue... BROTHER?' Zalbar glided to the altar and resumed arranging the journals. Fizbar felt faint, weak and soul-struck. 'Well, half-brother to be precise.'

Then a fire in the pit of his stomach shot to the surface. THAT'S A LIE!' he shouted at the top of his voice.

'I'm afraid it's the truth.' Zalbar kept his cool. 'Your look of stunned disbelief is actually quite entertaining.'

'You're nothing but a liar and a despicable traitor to all that wizardry stands for. Why should I believe a thing that leaves that pit of a mouth.'

'Learn that at school did you? Most amusing.' He crossed his arms. The Lex looked at each other, amazed at their Lord's self-control. Even they were surprised by the news. Gimera stood in the same position, he hadn't moved, nor did the expression on his face. 'Tell me youngling, why would I lie about something like that? What do I have to gain by revealing that I, Lord Supreme am related to a lowly FALZARD!' Zalbar's tone escalated, his voice coarse and grated.

The blaze in Fizbar's stomach had died down as his eyes began to well. His shoulders slumped and he lowered his spoon. He didn't have any energy left for any more surprises. He felt all had been lost. It was then that he knew why he was a Falzard. He had been punished by magic for the wrongs of his family. It was time to give up.

'Your mother and my father, well, let's not get into specifics. I was the first to be born out of their "friendship". Your father Jack found out. That's why he confronted my father, Rufus.' Zalbar opened his journal. 'So... BROTHER... It's time for a farewell despite this little family reunion.' Zalbar gestured to Gimera who moved for the first time. The Lex Talionis accompanied the Archmage, and the line was strong. Fizbar didn't know what to do, but he knew that it was not in his nature to give up so easily. Being a Falzard had taught him one thing and that was to be strong and to believe in himself. He dug deep into his soul for answers. He had to do something. Anything.

21

Battle at Filtzer Forest

The night air was now colder than before; a crisp breeze rustled through the treetops and swept across the grassy ground. Fizbar's fingers were numb and his toes felt like icicles. His mind felt oddly disconnected from his actions even though his head ached and his limbs seemed to be working without conscious instruction. Fizbar clutched his wand tightly, and smiled at his magical connection, however strange it was. He knew of only one way to end this with any slight chance of success.

'I challenge you to a duel!' Fizbar announced. 'Surely you can't refuse the old ways… Brother!' It pained him to speak the last word; it was visible on his face even though it was an attempt at sarcasm.

Zalbar stopped, but didn't turn. 'You are no match for me, and you are no wizard. You're a mistake. Thankfully, due to you I get to become Wizard Supreme, not our mother.'

'Are you refusing a wizard's request, dishonouring our

laws and values?'

'My dear boy, your codes and values are none of mine. Look at you.'

Fizbar fixed his eyes on Zalbar with a deep loathing.

'You're nothing but a wash-up. Those values of which you speak died out a long time ago. I haven't met a worthy contender even to this day.' He nodded in Therolius's direction; his eyes darting around like a crazy compass, 'Based on that, I shall consider your request as no request... Void.'

'Just like your face then,' Fizbar replied. He held his spoon loosely, ready for battle, but terrified.

Gimera's eyes widened. For once he reacted, glancing back at Zalbar who was still and silent. Meedril glanced at the staff; his look of panic could not have been a bigger giveaway. Meedril knew what he wanted to do.

Zalbar turned swiftly; his green cloak delayed coiling round the lower half of his torso.

'*Taciturnitas!*' A thunder of white light burst from his wand and shot at Fizbar. Another light shot from Fizbar's spoon just as quickly but it didn't hit the evil wizard. The force of Zalbar's bolt hit Fizbar in the centre of his chest throwing him backwards. He landed on the grassy floor and didn't move. Hetty waited in anticipation, hoping he would get back up immediately, but he didn't. She ran from the cover of the bush and knelt beside him. He lay motionless and cold on the ground. She stared into his brown eyes that were wide open. His pupils were large and fixed. A tear crept down her face. Just as she had begun to like him he had been taken away. Stroking his face she pleaded for his return. More tears followed, as she wiped her eyes. Gildor nervously flashed back and forth wondering what to do, startled. Gimera moved closer with his men, which made Gildor tense. The sweat started to run down his forehead. Gildor realised he was close to the altar. He could see Therolius, motionless next to Helena.

'Should have got rid of you a long time ago. You've only lasted because of Therolius. Look at him now. He's not here to help you and solve your problems. You're on your own!' Gimera raised his wand.

Gildor panicked, it was hopeless. He couldn't take on the Archmage. He was too strong. For a moment he thought hard, and reflected on Fizbar's journey: From a clumsy falzard, to an admirable wizard taking on a powerful evil. Surely he could do the same. After all, it was only words and rankings that distinguished their abilities, not the competence. He swallowed hard, plucked up the courage and performed a strange wizarding stance. They circled, and Gimera began to laugh. The Lex closed in on Gildor until finally Gimera gestured them to stop. They formed a circle.

'What in earth's name is that?' asked Gimera. 'Don't tell me you've been reading those hopeless stance books.

They don't improve your spell-casting.'

'We'll see about that won't we?' replied Gildor.

Meanwhile, Therolius suddenly felt a tingling in his limbs. He could move his fingers, then his head a little. Gildor noticed it from the corner of his eye, but Zalbar was unaware of it, concentrating on his journals. He opened his binding journal and ran his bony finger down its pages, muttering to himself like a mad man. Therolius was able to move his legs and his head a little more without raising suspicion. Helena followed his movements with her eyes, but she still couldn't move. He felt the spell wearing off, and then he could move his waist.

Zalbar began the incantation. Therolius felt it all coming back again. Long ago with Feena and his son Jack. The stars in the sky vanished and cotton swirls began to glow, lighting up the ground. Gildor looked up, as did everyone else. Even Hetty peered into the sky. Rain fell lightly like fine spray and distant thunder filled the sky like a roaring lion. The pounding thunder drew closer and closer. Hetty looked up and then to the edges of the forest. It appeared the thunder was not coming from the sky. Or was it? Flashes sparkled above, and then swirling lights lit the sky. Zalbar was shouting an incantation nobody understood. A golden aura navigated around his body before totally covering him. His wand unlatched from his skeletal hand and it hovered out in front of him within grasping distance. A green ray of light coated his wand. Therolius moved his head and noticed Zalbar's skeletal hand now had flesh. He instinctively looked at the face, but that was still the same. Nothing was there. His incantation became louder, and all the journals shone a variety of colours. Therolius managed to break free, but he realised his wand was nowhere to be seen. Zalbar observed Therolius, but continued with the incantation. He then looked at Meedril, who looked again at the staff. Zalbar nodded giving him permission. As he picked up the staff ready hit Therolius, a thumping noise from the forest broke though. Masses of hunchbacks entered with Nimvar at the front pointing a mace at the altar. He let out a guttural roar. Horns filled the sky and Nimvar rushed forward.

'MEEDRIL! DON'T YOU DARE!'

Meedril heard the voice and whispered, *father?* Then he withdrew and ran away into the depths of the forest.

Zalbar growled at his hunchback's betrayal, but it didn't stop his chant. Therolius turned his attention to Helena, but kept a watchful eye on Zalbar.

The Lex left Gimera and ran towards the hunchbacks. As they did, their bodies divided, then again, and again. Soon there were many Lex Talionis and the forest was lit with lights, fire and ice that shot from their wands. Gildor was now confronted with Gimera who had unleashed a range of bolts from his wand. Gildor managed to parry them, but noticed his adversary's strength.

Hetty stroked Fizbar's face. 'Don't leave us, Fizbar.'

Upset, she raised her head in the direction of her mother, and noticed Therolius was with her. She looked back at the young wizard and removed his hat, and then combed his hair with her fingers. A tear fell as she lowered her head towards his cheek. 'We all need you,' Hetty whispered. Suddenly her medallion began to glow. So did Fizbar's, then the aura expanded to his body. His wand lay next to his outstretched hand; it began to change to green. Hetty peered into his eyes and his pupils shrank. He let out a feeble cough and gradually came around, gasping for air. He wheezed a couple of times and Hetty pulled him close, squeezing him with affection before immediately releasing him, and standing up. Fizbar winced as he realigned The Grimoire that was digging into his back.

'My mother,' Hetty pointed. 'I have to…go.' She gestured again, this time a little red-faced and embarrassed.

Fizbar got up and grabbed her hand thanking her and smiled, but this quickly faded when he saw Gildor in battle with Gimera. There was an array of exchanging firelights as they flicked their wands at each other. Then Fizbar noticed Therolius next to Zalbar. It was strange. Therolius didn't seem bothered about Zalbar. Fizbar growled at the evil wizard and began to run towards him. He thrust forward his wand and noticed both his and Zalbar's wand was the same lustrous green. Then Zalbar's hand was forced open as his wand hovered out in front of him, only connected by a little strand of green thread-like light.

'What's happening, Thurrock?' Fizbar asked his wand, but there was no reply. 'THURROCK! WHAT'S HAPPENING?' he asked again, but again nothing. Instead he felt a warm glow on his back, as though a hot water bottle had been put there. He realised it was The Grimoire.

Therolius searched for his wand, feeling around the altar, grabbed it and pointed it at Helena. '*Exsolvo!*' he shouted and a force of wind left his wand. Helena slowly began to regain movement. The Overlord then turned his wand towards Zalbar. Fizbar shouted for him to stop, and momentarily he lost his focus. Zalbar turned his wand arm and a ray of fine golden light hit Therolius, sending him flying over the altar, high into the air. Zalbar laughed and the loud notes echoed into the darkness. Even Nimvar looked above and around him. Helena had managed to slide off the altar and away from Zalbar's control. Zalbar looked down and shouted at Gimera not knowing that he had still not defeated Gildor. Instinctively Gimera turned, losing concentration a fraction of a second. This was all Gildor needed and he pushed harder with his spell. Gimera looked back, but it was too late. His wooden face changed and a smile crept onto it before he burst into flames leaving only ash that wafted into the cold air. A weakened Gildor immediately ran to the aid of the hunchback's and found Nimvar. The Lex Talionis had summoned Arctodi and the bear-like creatures appeared in vast numbers.

Nimvar shouted to his kin. 'FOCUS ON THE LEX! ONLY THEN WILL THE ARCTODI FALL!'

Gildor saw sense in the hunchback's words and chose to fight the many Viktors and Hex brothers. The hunchbacks fought hard. Some with swords, others waving torches and clubs, whilst some preferred their bare hands. Many fell but so did the Lex Talionis and Arctodi. It was difficult to see if they were the real Lex Talionis or not. An Arctodus scratched Nimvar's arms and he let out a fierce roar. Then more hunchbacks joined from the trees, in aid of their leader. The Lex Talionis glanced at each other, for the first time a little worried, noticing their numbers dwindling. More armoured hunchbacks appeared, and others with rags that only clutched to their skin. The forest clearing was now full of hunchbacks.

Fizbar shouted at Zalbar who was muttering. He turned to face him, but couldn't speak, still locked into the incantation. '*Effligo fictum!*' Fizbar shouted again. Nothing happened. Zalbar narrowed his brow at him, noticing a little laughter in his incantation. With his wand still pointed at Zalbar he shouted again, '*Effligo fictum!*' Nothing happened. Then Fizbar realised. Both of their wands were hovering from their bodies. He closed his eyes and thought hard about the obliteration spell. Absorbing every letter and meaning of the spell. He stood there calm. Zalbar raised his hands and the sky turned emerald green.

His incantation was coming to an end. He slowly swivelled round and pointed his wand at Fizbar. He opened his eyes and noticed that the evil wizard's wand was dissolving. Then Fizbar's eyes flashed yellow like a granther, as he thought the spell... *Effligo fictum.* A red flame shot from his hand onto his wand, and then it blasted Zalbar. The red light attacked his golden aura and began to eat away at it like a virus. Zalbar gestured a moment of worry. Then in an act of rage he thrust his wand hand at Fizbar, but nothing happened. He attempted it again looking at his hand, as if it were a jammed gun. Zalbar began to wail. Flames swirled his body. He thought for a way out or a counter spell, but it was no use. He shouted and screamed. Then a face appeared where previously there had been just a void. It was the boy who had grown up. *'Brother,'* he whispered.

'You're no brother of mine!' replied Fizbar. Then Zalbar's body turned white and imploded. It had all happened so fast. The sky turned to night, and then the stars returned. The Lex Talionis burst into black-liquid smoke and vanished like their leader, but something told Fizbar that they would be back. With the Arctodi gone cheers escalated through the field. Gildor slumped to the ground in exhaustion and Hetty ran towards her mother. Fizbar searched a while for Therolius until he finally found him. He bent down beside him and rolled him over on his back. Fizbar sat down beside him, but unlike the rest he was far from happy.

'Master?' his wand finally spoke.

'Now you're talking? Why didn't you help me when I needed you?' he asked sourly.

A groan and Therolius opened his eyes and began to move. Fizbar helped him to sit up, along with a few moans and groans. They both sat on the damp ground, and this time it didn't bother Fizbar.

'Thurrock couldn't hear you. He was about to become obsolete.'

'He nearly did!' Fizbar agreed.

'Are you all right?' he asked the Overlord with heightened concern.

'I'll live if that's what bothers you.'

Fizbar fixed the Overlord's hat and helped him with his cloak and helped him to his feet.

'Come my boy. We've got a lot of catching up to do.'

They both smiled and joined the rest, as the hunchbacks continued to wave their torches in triumph. However, Fizbar still wondered about The Grimoire's part in what appeared to be a very happy ending.

22

Thurrock's Secret

It had been a week since the vanquishing of Zalbar. The Sintarian's were a happy people once again and trade was already starting to pick up. News had travelled far and wide and the Council had requested that Fizbar attend a Council meeting. He hoped he would advance a little more than just to second rank, and wondered whether he would join the Order of Light.

As he sat behind his desk the young wizard's elbows stretched far across the table. The thought of Therolius as his grandfather was still distressing, and he wondered if his surname would change. Would he now be known as Fizbar Delrunt? What warmed his soul was the thought of meeting Hetty later at her mother's shop. The Council had worked hard to get Helena's shop back to pristine condition and Hetty was taking him on an outing to the "Pickled Hen", which would involve song and dance… And pickles. Fizbar pondered on the prospect of Gildor's promotion to Archmage after the Council had nominated him making him the clear favourite. He wasn't sure if Gildor would want it, but hoped he would accept given the opportunity. A warm smile beamed from his pale face, and it sat there for a while.

'There's something that's been bothering me since that night in the forest,' said the wand.

'So now you're speaking to me?' Fizbar stated as the smile plummeted.

The wand didn't answer.

'Back to the silent treatment?'

'No.'

'Well that's a relief. I tell you. You have been really strange. It wasn't long ago that I couldn't shut you up.'

Again no reply.

'There's something I haven't told you,' said Fizbar.

'And that is?'

'Do you know that Nimvar had us followed? I wondered how he knew we'd be at the forest, but it turns out they were watching us all the time. They have kept an eye on that place ever since the revolt!' Fizbar poked the spoon. 'Just goes to show that they were the good guys after all,' he added.

'That's not what's bothering me.'

'What is it then?'

No reply.

'Thurrock, I wish you would just spit it out!'

There was a pause. Fizbar was completely attentive and

he tapped the wand again. 'Speak!'

'I used to be Mersden's magical guide.'

Fizbar grunted, but chose to react very calmly. 'How would you know that?' He said in a low tone. His wand was the only item on his wooden table. It lay facing him. Fizbar crossed his arms.

'Remember the visions?' said the wand.

'Yes.'

'It wasn't The Grimoire or because of your being a pure-blood. It was me.'

'What do you mean it was you?'

'I was channelling the visions to you. I was the conductor. Every time you had a vision, I was with you, literally stuck to you. I had visions too. Yet, for some reason still unknown to me, I couldn't tell you. That's why I've been…'

'Quiet!'

'Yes.'

'That still doesn't explain why you assume it was you.'

'Remember when you had all the visions by touching The Grimoire?'

'Yes.'

'I had some too.'

Fizbar didn't reply.

'They were all about Mersden for some odd reason. I realised that I was his wand in the visions. I used to be *his* magical guide!' Thurrock seemed distressed.

Fizbar got up and went to put on the kettle. He waited until it began to boil.

'Did you hear me?' The wand raised his tone to be heard above the whistling kettle.

'YES!' Fizbar snapped. He walked back after a few minutes with a steaming cup of green bubbling tea in his hands. 'I know.'

'What do you mean, you know?' the wand spurted out.

'Because the vision I saw also involved Mersden.'

'You mean…'

'Hmm. The visions about where the Overlord and Helena were being held; the hunchbacks; the battle of the past and present. It was Mersden who showed me everything through you and not the book. He showed me flashes of the past with him fighting alongside a younger Therolius.' He sipped his tea. 'Mersden couldn't kill his only son Rufus, what father could. When Rufus killed Jack, he realised he had lost his dear friend. He thought highly of Therolius. Looking at what Feena was doing and his son Rufus he couldn't decide what to do. He took the easy way out. He thought that if Rufus saw his father's death he would realise what he'd done, what he'd been involved in. He felt that Therolius would end his son's life for him.'

'But Therolius is not like that.'

'I know that, but Mersden didn't. When he saw Therolius holding Jack, he'd never seen that side of him before. He had to kill his son, but he couldn't. So…'

'He killed himself.'

'Yes, but what Therolius didn't know is that Mersden performed a spell that tied his soul and guide to The Grimoire. Mersden was the true protector of The Grimoire. He showed us both what he needed to know. It's because of him we managed to get to the forest in time.'

'The glow in the Overlord's office was…'

'Mersden, yes. Without you my friend Mersden wouldn't have been able to show me anything. There is one thing that puzzles me come to think about it,' said Fizbar, placing his cup on the coaster.

'What's that?' Thurrock asked with eagerness in his tone.

'If you were Mersden's magical guide, why didn't you bring some of that wealth of knowledge with you?'

'Maybe it's because he wanted us to grow together.'

Fizbar didn't detect the faint mocking. 'Yes, I get that, but how did he actually manage to get you to be *my* magical guide? That's the question.'

They both pondered in silence.

'Maybe it was part of another spell he cast? Or maybe one of those questions about magic we shouldn't know the answer to?' said Fizbar.

'Maybe you're right,' considered the wand. 'There's also another thing?'

Fizbar took off his hat and scratched his head. He placed

it next to his wand. 'What is it?'

'Zalbar was your… You know?'

'Yes.'

'Did you know when he was born, or anything else about him? I mean he just declared he was your, you know.'

'Yes.'

'Isn't that odd?'

'Gildor told me everything a couple of days after the forest fray. He told me that Feena didn't want Zalbar. Rufus wasn't bothered either. It was Gimera who took him to the orphanage. Gimera was the closest thing Zalbar had to a father, but somehow Zalbar still admired Therolius. Even more than Gimera.' Fizbar took a long sip of tea then picked up the feather, dusted, and then stared at his certificate on the wall. 'I'll tell you one thing, Thurrock.'

'And what would that be Master?'

'The world would be utter chaos without wands.'

'I agree. We also need wizards to maintain a healthy balance.'

'True. There's also something else.'

'Let me guess, that there is room for another certificate on your wall?

'Not a bad idea, but no.'

'That you may never become Overlord?'

'Never say never, but no, not that.'

'Then what is it?'

'Just that they don't teach you everything in school, do they?' He gave it another clean.

Acknowledgments

I have walked a long and winding path towards getting my first novel into print, but it has been a wonderful and enlightening journey. There has been numerous edits, "screen-glare" headaches, and painful revisits in refining the format of the book. But again, it's been worth it.

I am eternally grateful to Mark Iles for his kind words and support, sharp editing and proofreading skills, and especially his aid with formatting the manuscript.

I'd also like to thank Jonathan Bull for his skills and assistance with design and layout, without whom I would not be in print. I am eternally grateful to my own family and friends for their undividing support and faith in me as a writer, as well as a dreamer.

Lastly, but most importantly, I'd like to personally thank all of you who purchased the book, as well as the eBook. Without you all, getting this far wouldn't have been possible.

Independent Authors

Today's independent authors need every pinch of support. If you liked this novel then **please** spend just a little more of your time with a review, or recommend this novel to a friend.

Thank you for your support.

You can follow Jason on Facebook and Twitter.

 @jasonkurteaster

 FaceBook.com/JKEasterAuthor